Crazy Buffet Club

The BBQ Edition

A Second Helping Of Stories

Copyright 2019 by JimmyLee Smith

Introduction copyright 2019 by Calvin Beam

ALL RIGHTS RESERVED

No portion of this book may be reproduced in any form without permission from the publisher, except as permitted by U.S. copyright law. For permissions contact: info@crazybuffet.club

"Aftershocks" by Calvin Beam. Copyright 2019 by Calvin Beam. Printed by permission of Calvin Beam.

"Famous People" by Calvin Beam. Copyright 2019 by Calvin Beam. Printed by permission of Calvin Beam.

"Frost in the Sunlight: A Tale of the Winter's War" by Elijah David. Copyright 2019 by Elijah David. Printed by permission of Elijah David.

"Grandmother Moon" by Elijah David. Copyright 2019 by Elijah David. Printed by permission of Elijah David.

"Frank's Wheelbarrow" by Gary Sedlacek. Copyright 2019 by Gary Sedlacek. Printed by permission of Gary Sedlacek.

"Mama Oya" by J. Smith Kirkland. Copyright 2019 by J. Smith Kirkland. Printed by permission of J. Smith Kirkland.

"Happy Mother's Day" by Jerry Harwood. Copyright 2019 by Jerry Harwood. Printed by permission of Jerry Harwood.

"Share Taxi" by Jerry Harwood. Copyright 2019 by Jerry Harwood. Printed by permission of Jerry Harwood.

"Girl in a Taxi" by Joe Petrie. Copyright 2017 by Joe Petrie. Printed by permission of Jean Petrie.

"According to Sherlock: A Bree Watson Short Mystery" by Kelle Z. Riley. Copyright 2019 by Kelle Z. Riley. Printed by permission of Kelle Z. Riley.

"The Mover" by Marcus Brian Bankstone. Copyright 2019 by Marcus Brian Bankstone. Printed by permission of Marcus Brian Bankstone.

"A Lumberjack Thing " by Riley C. Shannon. Copyright 2019 by Riley C. Shannon. Printed by permission of Riley C. Shannon.

"Two Blown Tires Means a Road Trip " by Riley C. Shannon. Copyright 2019 by Riley C. Shannon. Printed by permission of Riley C. Shannon.

Cover Art by Meredith Hodges-Boos

www.crazybuffet.club
www.instagram.com/crazyBuffetClub

Dedication

For our spouses, partners, families, friends and, unapologetically, to each other. Without the incredible support we receive from them – the encouragement, the space to work, the perfect suggestions – none of this would be possible. Thank you all.

Introduction

Once again, this crazy group of writers that meets twice a month to talk about writing and the writing life, and of course, to eat, created 13 stories that comprise this collection. Because we meet in a barbecue joint, this second collection is called "The BBQ edition." We are nothing if not accurate.

We come to this collection from different genres, styles and experiences, which makes it all the crazier and more fun. As a member of this club, I hope you enjoy this second book. If you find an author whose style you particularly like, who stirs your emotions with a phrase, who plants a story in your mind that you remember long after you've put the book aside, we'll call that a success.

Finally, our Hixson, Tenn.-based group will donate the profits from our sales, as we did last year, to the Young Southern Student Writers sponsored by the Southern Lit Alliance and University of Tennessee at Chattanooga's Department of English. Our donations helps offset the cost of the awards ceremony they hold each year.

Table of Contents

Dedication..4
Introduction...5
According to Sherlock: A Bree Watson Short Mystery.............7
   Kelle Z. Riley
Aftershocks...16
   Calvin Beam
Famous People..20
   Calvin Beam
Frank's Wheelbarrow..28
   Gary Sedlacek
Frost in the Sunlight: A Tale of the Winter's War..................32
   Elijah David
Girl in a Taxi..47
   Joe Petrie
Grandmother Moon...56
   Elijah David
Happy Mother's Day...66
   Jerry Harwood
A Lumberjack Thing...73
   Riley C. Shannon
Mama Oya...78
   J. Smith Kirkland
The Mover...104
   Marcus Brian Bankstone
Share Taxi...116
   Jerry Harwood
Two Blown Tires   Means Road Trip 139
   Riley C. Shannon
About The Authors..149

According to Sherlock: A Bree Watson Short Mystery

Kelle Z. Riley

Every great detective has a nemesis. Sherlock Holmes—for whom I was named—had Moriarty. I have the Red Dot. Trust me, there is more to the Red Dot than meets the eye. I'm a cat, but I'm not stupid. Far from it.

Since the Red Dot entered my life just about the time I was adopted by Dr. Bree Watson, I should probably tell you a bit about her and how we came to work together. I like Dr. Watson. She's smart. It took me less than two weeks to teach her to respond to my whims. That's more than I can say for my previous owner.

Dr. Bree immediately recognized my mental prowess and dubbed me Sherlock in honor of it. Fitting, as we were both trying to determine the identity of the person who murdered my former owner.

His death didn't upset me. Cats don't fall prey to Stockholm Syndrome. He rescued me from a kill-shelter cage only to hold me hostage in another cage—a hard-sided cat carrier that was my only private place in his cold home. He didn't care enough about me to give me a name. Mourn him? I think not.

Bree, on the other paw, I'd do anything for. From the day we met, she presented me with food, shelter, and warmth. I mean, fluffy pillows, toys, Tiny Tuna Treats from *The Barkery*, and a comfy spot on her bed—what more could a cat want? If she wanted to know who killed my former owner, I was more than willing to help her. Besides, I was pretty sure I had information that she could use. We became partners in crime solving. My feline senses can sniff out a dirty, rotten murderer like nobody's business. Getting her to understand what I'm trying to say? That's a little more challenging.

Through Bree, I've met lots of new people. Before her, I was a loner. Sometimes by choice, sometimes not. But she is a social creature—every time she comes home I catch whiffs of the new and interesting people she's been around that day.

My favorite new friend is the delivery man from Chong's Chinese Restaurant. He always has a bit of real shrimp in his pocket for me. It's so good, even I can't play it cool when he comes to visit.

A close second to the delivery man is my friend Detective James O'Neil. Most cops are born dog people. I remember that from my kitten days when my littermates and I used to run from them. But that's another story.

I met the detective when he rescued me from the dead man's home. His scent was all cat comfort—like the smell of a little old lady a whisker's width away from adopting one more cat. Hello, happiness! What more could a twenty-pound tabby want in a person?

Then he took me to Bree. I let them both know what I thought of that turn of events. Swatted a couple of knickknacks and put them in their place, I did. But before long, I realized I'd landed in high catnip. I had Bree wrapped around my dewclaw as quick as you can say *meow*. And since the detective is sweet on her, it won't be long before I adopt him, too. I would NOT object to him sharing our apartment from time to time.

As it is, Detective James comes to the house often. He's so taken with me that he visits whenever Bree is out of town. I think he regrets not taking me to live with him. Not that I'd ever consider leaving Bree—even though she abandons me frequently for pesky to locations around the world for her job. The times she is at home are the happiest times of my life.

Spy Matthew Tugood, on the other paw, smells like trouble. He stalks Bree like a feral cat after a mouse, inviting her in then pushing her away. Watching him makes the fur on my tail stand up. I swear if I still had front claws, I'd swipe the fake smile off his face. Instead, I bide my time and tolerate him. From a distance. But I have news for Mr. Up-To-No-Good. Bree only has room for one cat in her life, and that's me. Not some scoundrel like you who's probably thrown away eight of his nine lives. *I'm watchin' you Nogood.*

But I digress. I was telling you about the Red Dot. It appears randomly in our home, darting from place to place, and I know it is a precursor to danger.

How, you ask, do I know?

Seriously? Do you not watch TV? Once I learned to use the remote (which Bree conveniently leaves on the coffee table), I started watching a lot of TV during the day while Bree was at work. At first, I concentrated on cartoons until the animated mice got on my nerves. Then I switched to cooking shows. My Bree is a pretty good cook when she tries. While I prefer take out (remember my friend from Chong's?,)Bree has whipped up some good meals. And she's constantly creating treats for her human friends. Cupcakes aren't my thing, but I do like to twine my way around her ankles and keep her company while she bakes. And, if she'd only listen to me, I could teach her a thing or two about pastry dough. If the contestants on the *Cook For Your Life* show can manage it, my Bree could do it. If baking is a science, she's got it covered. After all, she is a chemist. I remember the time she created Pina Colada Chicken Strips. Those were yummy. And when she tried the batter on shrimp —well, I'd even rate her above Chong's for that effort. I even love when she pulls out her Grandma's recipe box to make dishes. One day she…

Right. The Red Dot.

As I was about to say, before we got sidetracked, I spent some days watching TV and eventually landed on a crime show channel. Since Bree and I solve mysteries, it was a natural fit. Even if Bree says they make a lot of basic science mistakes. They are not mistaken about the Red Dot.

Every time the Red Dot appears, someone is injured or dies. Once Bree started investigating murders, the Red Dot appeared in our home. I'm not going to lose her because she stepped in front of it. So I chase it. Usually, the dot runs from me. Sometimes it lands on me, but my reflexes are fast, and I'm more willing to take my chances with it than to let Bree be in danger.

You may think I'm paranoid, but danger does seem to follow Bree like a mangy dog looking for a handout. After I pointed her to an important clue about who murdered her boss, she put the puzzle together and guessed who the murderer was.

Unfortunately, she guessed a little too late—just as the murderer tricked her into opening our door. If not for my quick actions, Bree would have been a goner. If a previous owner hadn't taken my front claws, I'd have gone for blood, let me tell you. But using my back claws and teeth, I distracted the murderer long enough for help to arrive.

I may not like Mr. Nogood, but I owe him and Detective James for saving my person. One of them fired the shot that kept Bree alive.

What keeps me awake all day is the worry that Bree will run into a murderer, or worse the Red Dot, when I'm not there to protect her. Try as I might, she won't let me follow her to the place she calls work. And without me, she's vulnerable. And most of the times she's come face-to-face with murdering scum, I've been locked in our home. Thinking about those showdowns scares a life out of me.

Another thing I don't like is when Bree makes friends with other animals. As much as I like the Tasty Tuna Treats from *The Barkery*, I'm not at all fond of the dog smells on Bree's clothing when she comes home from a visit there.

The Barkery is a strange place. Part pet-treat bakery, part grooming salon, and all cat-spit crazy if you ask me. I've learned (it isn't eavesdropping if you overhear it while sitting in your person's lap) that the owners, Horace and Wendy Clark love all animals. At last count they owned a dozen or so dogs, I think. They teach the dogs to do everything from chasing geese on command to sniffing out drugs. In my opinion, it isn't that hard to train animals of the canine variety. Dogs are so needy they'd do almost anything for a pat on the head, a dog treat, or a tennis ball. But defend their humans from murders while waiting for the police? That's a cat thing. My thing. And—like all self-respecting cats, I'm too intelligent to do a human's bidding. I prefer training them to do my bidding.

But I can't train Bree to stay away from *The Barkery* and because she usually brings something home for me—last time it was a car-shaped fish treat called a "Catalike"—I relent and let her go there to visit.

One time when she came home from *that place*, she had a small bipedal creature in tow. She called it a capuchin. I thought it looked like a monkey. Whatever it was, it was a thief. I caught it trying to pilfer Bree's necklace—the one with the tiny camera that she wears when she's undercover. It dropped the necklace and ran, barely escaping as I pounced toward it. I chased it through the living room and up onto the top of a cabinet. It spilled its little bag of contraband in the process, and I guarded the stash until I was able to bring it to Bree's attention. She returned the purloined items to their owners. At least I think she did. She seemed very sure of who the items belonged to.

As I said, Bree and I make a good team.

Speaking of which, if she doesn't wake up soon, she won't have time to feed and pamper me before leaving for her other job. Personally, I don't see why she has to do anything other than spend time with me—

—I mean spend time doing my bidding. Of course that's what I mean. Cats like me don't crave their human's touch, even in that special spot on the side of my jaw and right behind my ear. Nope. And that soft and warm sound her voice takes on when she talks to me? I tolerate it as a human foible. I don't long for it like a kitten listening for its mother's *mew*.

I don't. And I don't feel a rush of pleasure when she walks through the door. For catnip's sake! Don't confuse my actions with any of those messy, emotional dog habits. I would never give up my prize spot on the couch to run and greet her when she walks in the door.

You think I care about her? Get real. I care about not having to train another human if she falls prey to the Red Dot. That is the only—I repeat only—reason I may, *on occasion*, run over to check her out.

Speaking of training, my bowl is empty, my stomach is empty and my human is not doing her job. Time for me to remind her of what's important. As soon as I jump up on this bed.

So far, so good. Now time to get her attention.

Tap. Tap-a-tappity-tap-tap.

I hate smacking her cheek with my paw like that but my Bree sleeps like the dead. *Wake up!*

Mreewww.

"Not now, Sherlock. It's too early." She rolled over, dislodging me from my perch on her shoulder.

Not cool, human. *Grroww!*

Serious action is required. There. Her foot, moving back and forth under the cover. Clearly, she's only pretending to sleep, and not doing a good job of it either. I could teach her a thing or two about pretending to sleep.

But first things first. I need to teach her a lesson about ignoring my summons. Let me get my back paws under me. Right. Left. Twitch the tail. Adjust right. Adjust left. Pounce position ready. A flick of the tail—was that Bree's nose I felt mid swipe? No worries. Weight to the back, front paws ready. Watch the target. And...

Pounce! Grab the foot. Roll, swipe at the lower leg with my back claws. Nip.

"Sherlock!" Bree sat up in a rush and pulled her knees under her chin. Silly human, thinking that is out of my reach.

No matter. She's up and moving, shooting me looks of irritation and muttering about me under her breath. I let her attitude slide. She's shoving her feet into slippers and heading to the kitchen, which is what I want. Soon she's working the can opener and preparing my breakfast like a good human. I twine around her ankles, praising her for doing her job. Humans need encouragement.

"Oh, now you're a loving kitty." She frowns at me, but I can sense she doesn't mean it. "Sometimes I think I'm your servant, opening cans for you and cleaning your box."

Purr. Purr-purr-purr-purr. She understands. I interrupt my purring praise to give her calf a head butt.

"Okay, okay," she says, rubbing the spot behind my ears as she puts the bowl on the floor within reach. "I love you, too, Sherlock."

Wait. I'm not admitting anything about love. It's bad for the human's training. I almost growl at her, but really, the Salmon Surprise is so tasty, and her fingers are scratching that spot that I can never quite reach, and her voice sounds soft and still a bit sleepy. It's one of those moments when life is good. She's allowed to love me.

I sneak a peek around the kitchen, checking to see if the Red Dot has appeared. So far, so good. I covertly glance over Bree, but no dot. Just a goofy smile.

We're safe. For now. So maybe I can get just one more thing from my Bree.

Meow. I give her the look that she interprets as "please," then turn my head to the side and softly mew again.

"Oh, fine, you big baby." She scoops me up—all twenty pounds of me—and I rest my belly against her chest. I burrow my head into that spot between her neck and shoulder. The one that smells like Bree. My human.

She hugs me close, and I reward her with a rumbling purr that vibrates along her skin and mine. Bree doesn't need to know this, but I wouldn't trade her for the world. Not even for a catnip and tuna filled mansion with a private jet and fully stocked pond.

I rest one paw on her other shoulder.

I love you, too, my human. My Bree.

Aftershocks

Calvin Beam

After all these years, the house still smelled of The Law. If James stood stock still in the hallway outside the office door and closed his eyes, he could detect notes of cologne, evening brandy, occasional cigars and heavy leather-bound books. The aromas from the kitchen at the end of the hall had been the first to disappear. And then the little perfume and potpourri scent of Nanny, who lived in the room next to the kitchen and whose actual name James never knew, even after he had looked into her puffy red eyes and listened to her blow her nose into a linen handkerchief when they both realized there was no reason for her to stay on.

Even before attack, James's mother was a severe and silent woman. She moved catlike about the house in flat, soft shoes, with no jewelry to rattle, a cat with no bell. As a boy, he had always been afraid to look, but he was certain that when they went to the Jersey Shore she walked without leaving footprints in the sand. His mother withered away in a nursing home without complaint or comment. The attendants said she died from grief, but James knew grief was one of the many emotions she didn't have.

On his left was the sitting room that he was never allowed to use because children don't know how to sit without fidgeting and they always have dirt that transfers to expensive carpets and upholstered furniture. The room looked like a comic Klan meeting now, with white sheets draped over various pieces that needed to retain their value for the new owners. The agent, a bird-like woman both in chirpy movements and voice, told him the sheets were necessary and she would take on the responsibility of removing them each time there was a showing and replacing them when it was over.

His father's office was always off limits, too, even though it held a treasure trove of delights for a young boy. The heavy magnifying glass on the reading table. The enormous sepia globe that spun effortlessly in its walnut supports. The rolling ladder that moved noisily on casters along tracks and gave access to rows of books that were out of the reach of mere mortals. The room was arrogance in physical form. He had imagined being welcomed into the office when he became a lawyer, but the welcome never came.

A small barroom sat just off the formal dining room. James opened an inlaid wood humidor and the scent of aging cigars hit him like a guilty verdict. He still felt like a thief as he took one of the dwindling supply of Montecristos, then tucked it behind his black silk pocket square. He took a small old-fashioned key and unlocked the liquor cabinet, then removed the cork from a bottle of cognac and poured two swallows into a small traveling flask.

The Law would have lowered his head and looked disapprovingly over his rimless reading glasses at the casual way his long-cultivated vices were being treated.

James's cellphone played a muted orchestral phrase and even that caused him to jump. It was the agent.

"There's a very promising couple who wants to see the house. But they must see it today."

"No, not today," James said. "Maybe next week." He

disconnected.

It was two subway stops to the park. He used the time to think about his mother. In the end, all she gave him was money.

Fall hadn't yet figured out it was mid-September and the sun beat down while he climbed the hill. He was a city boy, and the emerald grass reminded him of baseball games under the lights at Yankee Stadium. He harbored a secret passion for New York's other baseball team, but The Law had laid down that respectable New Yorkers didn't root for the Mets.

James was sweating when he reached the place where the black wrought-iron bench sat. He believed this was why his father chose this spot, but James lowered himself and sat on the grass in his charcoal wool suit.

From his inner jacket pocket he pulled a leather case that held a steel guillotine cutter, a pearl-studded lighter and a nylon disposable ashtray. He prepared the cigar because it was one of the things his father couldn't do for himself anymore. He lit it and let the acrid smoke waft over him. He took a swallow of the cognac and faced The Law.

"I suppose you know the city taxes are killing me," James said. "We've had a number of offers for the house, but they never seem to be the right kind of people."

He let the sentence hang in the air. "I'll have to sell eventually. Perhaps you'll let me know when the time is right."

"Here's to heroes," James said, and he poured the rest of the brandy at the base of the marble stone engraved with his father's name and the dates, June 6, 1935-September 11, 2001.

He waited in silence until the cigar burned itself out. Then he wrapped it in the nylon and dropped it into a metal bin on his way down the hill.

Famous People

Calvin Beam

Albert Einstein

Einstein walked into the kitchen but forgot why. So he made a sandwich and went back to his study, where he worked on the general theory of relativity for .... he wasn't sure. Time is relative after all.

He heard a knock at the door and went to answer it. As he stood quietly and looked at the closed door, he wondered why he had come there. A second knock jogged his memory.

The knocker was a delivery man with a package inside a plastic bag. Einstein signed for it. The delivery man left and Einstein looked at the packing slip: "Caution: Medicine. Feline leukemia."

Einstein idly wondered if he had a cat he had forgotten about. If he did, it needed help. He scoured his rooms but there was no food, no litter box, no fur, no squeaky toys. By the time he concluded he didn't have a cat, the delivery man had driven away and Einstein was left holding the bag.

He looked for a return address. It was in Boston and he was in Vienna. That didn't seem practical even if the universe was curved to allow the two cities to touch.

He looked at the delivery address. "Apartment 4A."

He looked at his door. "Apartment 4C."

Then he had a flash of insight about mass and the speed of light and hurried back to his desk to work again before the thought left him.

A moment later, or it might have been two weeks, he heard a knock at the door.

That caused Einstein to remember the package and he took it to the door in the hope the delivery man might have returned.

Instead, there was a woman at the door. She was crying.

She brightened immediately when she saw the package. "Thank you, you're a life saver," she said.

"No, but I am a genius. Would you like to come in and see my theory?"

The woman hurried back to apartment 4A, convinced that Einstein was an odd and possibly perverted man.

Abraham Lincoln

Abraham Lincoln was sitting on the train when an older lady boarded and sat down beside him.

Lincoln was busily writing but that didn't stop the woman from saying hello.

Lincoln grunted in response. His guard stood to remove the woman, but Lincoln waved him away.

"Where are you headed?" the woman said. "I'm going to Chambersburg."

"Gettysburg," Lincoln said.

"I'm not sure I would go there right now," the woman said. "Terrible stench about the place. And all shot up. There isn't a decent hotel to be had."

"I won't be staying that long," Lincoln said.

The woman looked over Lincoln's arm to read what he was writing. He curved his hand to hide his work. "It's just a draft," he said.

"Aww, let me see," the woman said. "I won't make fun of it."

Lincoln sighed and handed over several sheets of paper.

"Hmm," the woman said. "You know, I'm a retired English teacher. Do you mind?"

She whipped out a blue pencil and began furiously making marks and scratching things out.

Lincoln looked at one of the passages.

"But, in a larger sense, we cannot dedicate—we cannot

consecrate—we cannot hallow—this ground, " he read. "Hey, that's pretty good."

She returned the papers. There was a lot of crossing out.

"There's not that much left," Lincoln said. "It's going to be too short."

"When someone gives a speech, there's no such thing as too short," the woman said.

Lincoln nodded.

"Oh, this is my stop," the woman said. "I didn't get your name."

"Abraham," Lincoln said.

"Too stuffy," the woman said. "You should go by Abe. And I would lose the top hat. You're already tall enough."

Queen Elizabeth

The lights went out at Buckingham palace and the queen was not pleased.

She waved in the dark for an aide. The man screamed. He was not used to the Royal We poking him in his non-royal eye.

"What is the meaning of this," the queen said.

"It's budget cuts," the aide said. "There is a cash flow problem."

"We are not amused," the queen said. "How can We fix it?"

"Might I suggest selling some of the accumulated palace bric-a-brac," the aide said. "It could be a like a royal lawn sale."

"A capitalist idea," the queen said.

When the sun came up, servants began to move items onto the lawn. There were gifts from foreign dignitaries, some royal baubles, a box of Churchill's cigars.

While the queen oversaw the setup, a servant pulled Prince Charles from the corner where he had been standing.

"What about him?" the servant said. He used a white cloth to brush some dust that had accumulated in Charles' hair and to flick some cobwebs from his ear.

"He'll never sell," the queen said, "at least not on his own."

"Maaybe we could put him on one of the thrones and make it a package," the servant said.

The queen guffawed. "No one will believe that. Here, put him behind this Louis XVI writing desk."

A customer appeared and began haggling. I like this writing desk. Can I get it without the prince chap?"

"Everything must go," the queen said.

Frank Sinatra

Frank Sinatra was sitting at the bar talking with Dean Martin. It was a cozy bar, somewhere on the Vegas Strip. It was late at night, or early in the morning. In the neon lights of Vegas you can only tell the difference by the redness of people's eyes.

A portly balding man walked by, accompanied by a statuesque blond woman. Martin gave a low whistle. The woman smiled at Dean, but the man just glared.

"Looks like you had good luck at the tables tonight, Clyde," Sinatra said.

"My name is Howard," the portly man said. "And I resent the implication."

It was Sinatra's turn to whistle.

"Did you ever notice," Sinatra said to Martin, "that the truly lucky guys are forever denying that luck has anything to do with it?"

"You mean like the fact that we can get jobs that let us drink until 4 a.m. and then sleep it off?" Martin said.

"Something like that," Sinatra said. "I mean, we must be the luckiest schmoes on the planet. Except for Clyde, here."

"Howard," Howard said curtly. "Look, not every woman is susceptible to flash and cheesy come-on lines. I met Sandra at an art gallery."

"I always get the brush off when I talk to girls at art shows," Martin said.

Howard pushed on. "We talked. Real conversation. I won her over with charm and personality, and she did the same with me. There is still room in this country for a man to act like a gentleman. Isn't that right, Sandra."

Behind Howard's back, Sandra held her two hands about a foot apart and opened her eyes as wide as they would go.

Sinatra and Martin both whistled.

"Now that's a gentleman and a half," Sinatra said.

"Two gentlemen, in my case," Martin said.

Howard smiled and he and Sandra walked away. Sandra turned to the boys and blew a kiss over her shoulder.

Frank's Wheelbarrow

Gary Sedlacek

On the small bench under a large cottonwood tree that shaded his father's gravesite, Frank slouched forward, both elbows on knees, head down, and clasped his hands. He lifted his head, looked at his father's gravestone, and said, "What's a soul?"

He dropped his head again.

"Karl and I were just now visiting in his bar and I asked him that because last night Irene said they've been talking about such things, and Alma too for that matter. Surprised me. Irene and I, we've been married eight years but we never talked about such things as souls."

Frank coughed and shifted his weight.

"You probably know all this already, but Irene caught me and Alma doing the deed last night and Irene was not happy. She didn't throw things. But she said I didn't have any soul. Maybe she's right. I couldn't sleep, and those windows in the house, even last night with a full moon shining on that fresh snow cover, those windows were dark. Irene said I was looking at the darkness in my soul and I couldn't see light until I cleaned my soul."

Frank shifted his weight again, unclasped his hands, lifted both of them, then let them hang limp from his wrists.

"So I came in town and asked Karl what a soul was, figuring

he, after talking to Irene and Alma about it, would give me some help."

Frank shook his head.

"He told me that to him 'soul' was like light that he saw through his telescope. When he looked through that 'scope of his he saw way more light than darkness and he said our souls were all that energy out there in human form."

Frank lifted his head and looked at his dad's gravestone.

"Alma says something like that. She says our souls are energy too, but a different kind of light than Karl says. Kind of like a glow of a lantern without the flame."

Frank sat back against the back of the bench and let his hands rest on his knees.

"And, you know, that's a lot like what Pastor Dietz says too. He says it is a kind of energy inside us that maybe we can see as a glow, like those halos in pictures of Christ and the angels."

Frank crossed his arms. "All those souls, Karl's, Irene's, Alma's, and Pastor Dietz', they all had to do with light. And last night I didn't see any light."

He frowned.

"I saw exactly the opposite. Nothing but darkness coming in where even natural light should have been. Am I so dark inside I can't even see moonlight off of fresh snow when it hits me in the face?"

Frank reached up with his right hand and rubbed his eyes. Then he dropped his hands to his lap. He shook his head.

"I can't be all that bad. Not that bad."

Frank looked at his father's gravestone.

"You and I never talked much. But this much you know. What is a soul? Do I have one? Can I find it if I've lost it?"

Frank looked up at the branches of the tree over his head.

"Why can't I feel anything?"

He leaned back so his head rested on the back of the bench.

"When I was a kid, you remember that corncrib we had with the windbreak behind it and you parked some of our farm equipment back there? There was this wheelbarrow and I just fit into it. I used to sit in it and my legs were long enough to hit the ground and the tall part of it was big enough to give me a head rest. I'd sit in that thing with my feet on the ground and my head leaned back with my eyes on the branches over me. I would look at the clear sky through the tall branches and I could feel the earth's energy come up through my feet and go out the top of my head. I was just buzzing - there was so much."

Frank looked back down at his father's grave.

"I must have had a soul then or I wouldn't have felt all that energy. Maybe that's what I should look for now?"

He scuffed aside the snow from the night before until he felt the ground under his shoe sole. He planted both feet firmly on cleared ground and leaned back with his head tilted upward to the branches and the clouds and the clearing sky, and waited. Nothing happened. He pressed harder with his toes to make firmer contact with the ground, then looked again up at the sky and waited. Nothing happened.

He quit trying.

He quit arching his neck and forcing his feet against the ground. He simply allowed his eyes to follow the land across the width of the Platte Valley, two and sometimes five miles wide. Across the Valley forming the trough between him and the far bluffs on to the high ground where his farm lay stretched a covering of fresh, white, clean snow just a few hours old, laced with trees following the river, with the river, dark and muted, even in the daylight that brightened the snow cover.

He settled into this scene. His torso, cushioned by his relaxing muscles, bent to a natural curve, like the river, and he felt the river's and the sky's and the trees' warming energy flow through him generating heat that filled his winter coat and gloves. He smiled. He knew he had something left, some little bit of energy all these other people must have meant when they talked about souls.

Frank looked at his dad's grave.

"Now I know I'm still connected with the land."

He stood.

"So that's it. That's me. That's what I'll stand for until I can't stand any more."

Frost in the Sunlight: A Tale of the Winter's War

Elijah David

Warm Hearts in a World of Ice

Jack Frost opens up about love, loss, and his friendship with St. Nick

-River Martin

Everyone knows his name, though few have claimed to see him. Fewer still have met him, though his handiwork is displayed around the world year after year.

When I arrive at the small, open-air bar Mr. Frost requested for our meeting place, I find myself once more surprised by his choice. The theme, fittingly enough for Oahu, is tropical; grass skirts and leis and fruity drinks with umbrellas, as cliche as a '90s sitcom. Despite the chill in the air driving the guests toward the relative warmth of the bar itself, the outer half-wall's vinyl sides are rolled away, per Mr. Frost's request.

He is seated on one of the stools that line the half-wall, his back to the bar, elbows jauntily leaned on the walltop. His features are simultaneously elfin and all too human. Sharp cheekbones offset a nose bent from fights, and hair too pale to be natural frames soul-dark eyes. Those eyes have seen unfathomable beauty and unmistakable horror, and a smirk hides to one side of his mouth that makes anyone who sees him wonder which will rule the day—beauty or horror.

"First things first," he says when we have formally introduced ourselves, "no questions about powers or realms or anything I don't feel like answering. Push too far and you'll find yourself without an interviewee—or a temperature."

He says this with a grin on his face, but the truth of the matter is that there are some subjects we can't discuss, even on the neutral territory he has selected. In the communications that precipitated this meeting, he laid out much the same guidelines, though in slightly more detail. And with slightly fewer threats.

I nod in agreement and, when he pushes for a more formal answer, reply, "Agreed. Only safe subjects."

He claps his hands together and rubs them like an actor in an old pantomime, ready for the thrill of the hunt or the challenge of matching his nemesis's wit.

"Excellent. Where shall we begin?"

I begin with the most obvious question, though not necessarily the one everyone else would ask.

"Is your name really Jack Frost?"

He laughs, a surprisingly warm sound that reminds those who hear it of burbling creeks in summer shade.

"It might as well be," he says. "They've been calling me that for so long, I'm not sure I'd answer to anything else."

So he can remember a time before there *was* a Jack Frost.

"Oh yes, but understand that it isn't like you remembering your childhood nickname or what you called your favorite teddy bear." He pauses, leaning back further against the half-wall and closing his eyes as if he must travel the halls of memory in truth as well as metaphor. "They were short, happy days. Not that there wasn't anything to be sad about. There's always something, you know? But there was more happy than sad. That's why we—why we're doing this."

His tone makes it clear that he is not referring to our interview. A moment later, he turns the conversation away from who the others in that mysterious *we* are and what their work might be. He has toed the line between safe and forbidden subjects and will not return to the brink so easily.

I ask about the media portrayals—television specials and movies and department store displays decking him out as a winter sprite with a heart as cold as stones under ice.

"If I had any say in that, I don't think we would have as many images of me in the world. Not because I wouldn't let them be made, but because people wouldn't be interested in the sorts of images I would make."

But people love his work when he visits frost on windowpanes and freezes the dew in spiderwebs.

"True, but they hate when I have to slick their roads with ice or overburden powerlines. There's little choice in the matter all around. So let the people have their fancies and their dreams. Even the darkest ones can't paint me worse than I've been."

Encouraged by the heat of the sun on my back, canceling the chill that had marked my arrival, I ask him to talk about that darkness. What has he done to make killer snowmen seem light by comparison?

He turns to face me with a questioning look on his face, brows furrowed in confusion, as though he has forgotten the last few moments and is trying to work out what we're doing here, what we're talking about.

"Oh," he says at last, "everyone has things about their past they'd rather forget, things they'd rather no one knew. Abandoned friends, hateful thoughts, thoughtless words." He trails off, letting the renewed breeze carry his words away. Half-whispering, he adds, "Old flames."

A flash of icy blue crosses his eyes, as of some forgotten fire stirring along with memories.

I ask if there was ever a Mrs. Frost.

"Who would want to be?" he asks, though the laughter that follows is as hollow as the wind. He shakes his head and stares toward the ocean, half-hidden behind high-rises and just distant enough to be drowned out by man-made noises. Then he begins to sing, soft and sweet like a chime, "Jack and Jill went up the hill to fetch a pail of starlight."

Despite the chatter of the bar, several other patrons turn to stare and strain for the words as he continues.

"Jill sat down and took up her crown. Now Jack is broken-hearted."

Though he sings slowly, allowing the notes to hang in the air like invisible snowflakes, the song ends all too quickly. The other patrons return to their drinks and their conversations. The magic cannot linger, no matter how subtle.

"It was true enough," Frost says, "when they first began to sing it. Oh, I was dark in those days. Not at first. No one ever starts out a midnight terror." He turns an appraising eye to me once more and says, "I am going to tell you a story I've never told anyone before. Perhaps you can print it, perhaps not. But it is worth sharing." He closes his eyes and for a moment, he is altogether human. His ears are not so fey, his face not so sharp. Then those eyes that have seen the abyss open again, a trace of blue fire at their edges. "It is right that someone else should know, if this be the last."

I must pause in my narrative to present his words as carefully as I may. Who can know if there is not some spell woven into them that would break if I should alter them for my own ends?

You must understand that I was broken-hearted. I had offered her all I knew to give, and more than I was certain I could give. It was all we could ever have wanted.

But some duties are greater than a person's heart or where it leads.

I did not leave her immediately afterwards. It would have been less painful if I had, but it would also have proven I was never worthy of her in the first place. And pride, or spite, or pure mule-headedness kept me from saving myself the agony of seeing her each day, knowing whatever we might have had was lost forever.

Eventually I could bear the reminder no more, and I sought some excuse to leave. I could go as an ambassador or a scout or a hundred other plausible but false missions that would keep me from her for a few centuries at least. In the end, none of them suited and I simply left.

It was not as hard at first as you might think. The first decades flew by in a haze of blizzards and mischief. Fewer folk died then than might have if I'd been more honest about what lay in my heart. I told myself I was free at last—from the pain, from her presence, from even the memory of our time together.

But freedom is not freedom if you must run from it.

And I ran in those days. I ran from pole to pole and back, an ever-moving whirlwind of frost and fancy.

I cannot say now what stopped me in my stirring, if it were some woodcutter working late in the season to feed his starving children or some kind-hearted soul nursing a sick husband. But some small moment of humanity arrested me, as easily as if I'd been a child in the market bedazzled by a shining trinket.

And fury awoke inside me. Rage like I had never felt before stirred in my icy chest, and I brought such a winter down upon these unimportant mites, these baleful little wastrels holding on to something warm and soft in my season of ice.

It lasted, oh, so many years. Not without break, mind, but with few and short enough that I might have been moved to press for something like eternity, if only it hadn't meant an end to humanity and thus an end to my rage's surrogate. I wanted to prolong their suffering as I had prolonged my own pain. Eventually my hold, my reign as it were, grew so sure that I retreated to a high and lonely place where I could watch the fruits of my labor freezing on the vine.

One night, as I sat in my lonesome sanctuary, he came to me. I would say it was midwinter, because that is his time, but that was such a long winter; I could not say it and be certain it was true.

You'll expect me to say he wore a red coat and laughed and tossed presents to every well-behaved child for miles around. But that's not Nick. Not for a long while before I met him. And he never did care for red. He's a green man.

He had put down his sword for a time. Peace on Earth, as they say. I wanted none of that. I howled and threw my fiercest winds to blow him away from my retreat. They did not move him. Even then, he'd had centuries to learn patience and stolidness. I doubt even the devil could stand long against Nick when his mind was bent to a task.

And that night, his mind was bent on me.

People sing about how he sees you—awake, asleep, bad, good—as though it's just another person noticing that you got your hair cut or how nice you look in that blouse today.

They don't know what it's like to have something as old as Nick focused solely on you.

I'd say something about ice running down my spine, but that would be in poor taste. Truthfully, when my winds didn't shift Nick from his goal, a wave of uneasiness like an early thaw spread through my gut. But I tried one last time to deter him, to alter his route to one side or the other. In the end, he reached me and put his hands around my wrists.

Have you ever been in a snowstorm? Have you seen the world shaken up like a snowglobe and then suddenly the wind stops and everything is still—so quiet and unmoving that for a heartbeat or two you wonder if you've gone deaf or the world has ended and this is all that's left—you and the streetlight and half a foot of snow suspended in the too-thick air?

Imagine being the one in charge of the storm, and having that same pause be forced upon your charge.

Nick's strength was surprising enough that I didn't try to resist. I simply surrendered out of shock. He took me aside—quite a way aside, if I'm honest, but that's not really a clear way of explaining. Let's just say his steps went further than yours would. Then he told me why he'd come. Or he tried to.

"Ror's using you to do her dirty work now, is she?" I asked.

"Is it a black deed to turn aside the wrath of another?"

I didn't meet his gaze. I wanted none of his righteous chatter. He was infectious, a plague of good cheer and merriment that could spread like wildfire through you and all you knew if you hesitated even a moment.

"I don't want it turned aside," I said, casting about for an avenue of return. I hadn't seen exactly the steps he'd taken to bring us away from my sanctuary, and without that knowledge I was as stranded here as any human in one of my blizzards.

"Clearly," said Nick. "But it is rare that one in the grip of anger wishes to be released. Especially anger as long-lived and well-fed as yours."

"Then you admit your cause is hopeless," I said. I risked matching him eye for eye. "You may as well leave me to it. Take me back." I waved my hand in what felt like the proper direction, but who knew in what direction home truly lay.

"My cause is never hopeless," he replied, with all the quiet dignity of a king weathering a tantrum from his spoiled heir. "You used to believe that."

"I believed many things wrongly, Nicholas. Why should this matter be any different?"

Though his attention never wavered from me, he turned

outward to gaze at the night sky, as dotted with stars as a field under a new snowfall. Truthfully I felt I would rather let the force of his mind carry me where it will, but that same prideful desire to prove him wrong kept me upright and I glared at him and the view, seeing neither beauty nor hope.

When Nick spoke again, it was like the whisper of a hearth in the longest night. "She worries for you."

I wasn't aware of the daggers of ice I'd sent flying at Nick's back until I saw them suspended millimeters from his robe. He hadn't had to wait that long to stop them, nor had he been forced to keep their shapes. He had done both for my benefit, and the first drip of a thaw traced its way down the surface of my heart.

"'I will love you till the moon burns down.' Those were the words of our troth, Nick. Ror broke those when she chose the crown over me."

"It wasn't as simple as—"

"Of course it was simple!" The night sky had vanished behind a flurry of snowflakes as thick as any blizzard I had ever spent on the humans, the stars erased by a closer, colder whiteness. "We were going to leave it all behind us. We could have been—"

"I know," he said. There was a surprising lack of comfort in his voice, as though he would not waste pity on someone unwilling to respond. Good. That meant I was wearing him down. He wouldn't try much longer to persuade me.

"Then you know I am in the right."

His brilliant eyes flashed on me, like beacons of another world brought to bear on my existence. "'In the right,' Jack?

How is it right to vent yourself on those who have done you no harm, to starve and kill and torture beings whose lives you could improve?"

"I'm part of winter. They bring their fires and their songs and their animal skins to bear against me and mine and yet they can make no lasting mark upon us. How do I improve their lives?"

Between heartbeats he was at my side once more, his hand clenched as tightly around my wrist as any manacle. "Come," he said, command dripping from his voice like spring melt. Then his grip shifted and he was taking my hand as if we were old friends meeting on the street. "Come," he repeated, "and see."

We stepped sidelong again, and in my astonishment I failed to see the steps once again. We were in a place that seemed familiar this time; some human community along a river. I had visited it many times in my self-imposed exile, but never lingered longer than was necessary to give it a thorough frosting. Even in my harshest winters, I did not give one town preeminence over others.

Snow—my snow—covered everything not warm enough to melt it or well-trodden enough to transmute it into slush. Ice crept in beneath the snow in many places. Everywhere we turned, my winter encroached upon the humans, and all of their weapons against it—fire, movement, gathering together— could hardly hold it back or slow its advance.

"I fail to see—" I began.

"That much is evident," Nick said. He did not guide me as one human might have guided another through that treacherous labyrinth of slick cobblestones and icy alleyways.

He simply moved us from place to place, darting us in an indirect manner toward the river at the heart of the city.

I say the river lay at the heart, because regardless of human borders and boundaries, the water always draws centricity to itself. And this city was no different.

But where I expected to see a tundra of ice and snow dividing the city, with perhaps a few huddled migrants scattered around a pitiful attempt at warmth, I saw something entirely different.

They were happy. Amidst all my ice and snow and mournful frost, they had constructed a fair. A carnival. A means of beating back the despair I had nurtured in my heart for years of their time.

Stalls lined the river on both banks, and even stretched out onto the frozen surface. The aromas of spicy meat mingled with sugary pies and roasting nuts. Laughter and shouting and even some off-key singing rang across the open air like bells in a wild chorus.

I felt anger rising in me again, burning like frostbite, but Nick's hand hung heavily on my shoulder and the storm I'd been ready to send tearing through their festivity died before I could summon a single snowflake.

"You see," said Nick, "even in the harshest of winters, they can find hope."

It was a typical Nick perspective. It elided the starving children and freezing beggars on the edges of the fair. Yet even as I thought it, I knew I was being overly critical. Nick would not be Nick if he didn't *see the children and beggars and all the other misfortunate among the throng below. That was who he was, after all. The hope-kindler. The joy-bringer. The merry-maker.*

Nick knew who he was. Always had, as far as I was aware.

Meanwhile, I didn't know who I was. Not anymore. Not since Aurora broke my heart.

I had thought I could be a frost demon, the bane of these puny humans and their fleeting existences. But I had failed in that. Even if in no other place on this globe people gathered to hold back the cold and the dark, this place would always stand as a testimony to my failure. I would never be able to erase it from my memory, just as I could never erase Ror's decision to leave me for her crown.

I turned to Nick and found him waiting, patient as Time, stern as a cliffside, merry as—as himself.

I had forgotten the strength that comes with being merry. It goes deeper than a happy hour or two and digs into the bones, taking root in the very soul of a person, and nourishes them through the hard times like a cactus weathering the desert sun.

"I've been a fool," I said at last.

"Art wiser than most fools, for few ever have the strength to admit their foolishness."

We stood there much longer, unobserved by the humans around us. The sun set and the fair dispersed, though not for long. Before dawn the workers and tradesmen and hawkers would be back to do the whole thing over again. And all through the night, not so clear and starlit as in that other place, but still beautiful in its way, we stood above the river, waiting.

Waiting.

Waiting.

Back in the bar, I wait for Mr. Frost's words to pick up. For more than half an hour, we sit in a silence much like the one he and Nick stood in those centuries ago. He is clearly referring to the Frost Fairs of London, or some similar festivity. How must it be to have watched so many ages of human culture pass by? What stories could he tell if only we knew the questions to ask?

But of course the question that breaks the silence has nothing to do with human history.

Did he go back to her?

For a moment, Frost's eyes are ringed with blue fire, but whatever emotion that blaze signals he suppresses. When he speaks, he says only, "No. I couldn't."

Wasn't that why Nick had come? To bring an apology, a chance for reunion? Or had he simply come to end Frost's wintery war on humanity?

With this last line of inquiry, Frost stands and brushes his immaculate white pants with the palms of his hands.

"I believe this interview is over," he says.

Questions come flooding so quickly they choke each other and none escapes, save for one, the least important of all.

How did such a small effort on Nick's part change the course of Frost's life?

"I said the interview is over," Frost says, his namesake spreading across the half-wall of the bar, the stools on either side of us, the sand at our feet. "But here is one final observation for you: if you ever meet Nick, you'll wonder why it took so much effort for me to change."

He leaves, the frost vanishing in the moderate heat of the day. He does not dissolve or disintegrate. There is no fancy side-stepping or dramatic snap of the fingers. He simply walks away from the bar like any normal human might, a trail of frosted footsteps lingering momentarily in his wake.

I watch him leave, knowing I have pushed further than I ought, yet unable to bring myself to regret asking the questions that have driven him off, in my mind, prematurely.

Where he has gone, I cannot say, but I guess he has gone back to the fight. Though he cannot speak to the matter by choice or by oath, Jack Frost is a member of some furtive group of figures who are waging a secret war. This war is fought not over territory or resources or wealth, but over the hearts, minds, and I dare say the souls of humanity.

They stand at the heart of winter, a time when the threats of despair and hopelessness are at their zenith, and they push back against the dark tide. They kindle joy and hope, delight and wonder, in a time when we need them most.

Among this group stands Nick, known more broadly as Saint Nicholas, or Santa Claus, or any of a hundred other names. Aurora, Jack's lost love, must surely be the leader of this band of encouragers, though she has not always been. "Jill sat down and took up her crown," Frost said.

I believe what happened that night when Nick showed Jack the resilience of the human spirit was this: Nick saved Jack from the frozen despair they also strive to save us from. In the end, their mission is more important than whether Jack and Aurora found a happily ever after with each other. They are fighting for our happiness, after all.

Though a none-too-small part of me hopes for them to rekindle that flame someday.

Publishing this article may bring unwelcome attention from those against whom Nick and Frost struggled. Certainly it will bring scorn and derision from my peers. But that cannot be helped. I have met Jack Frost and heard his story, and for me to keep silent about it would do both of us a disservice.

Some causes outweigh personal desire.

Girl in a Taxi

Joe Petrie

I watched her hesitate and then point to the large chocolate-chip cookie in the display case. She turned and looked up at me. At ten she had Deb's sky-blue eyes magnified by the round glasses balanced on her short turned-up nose.

"You sure?" I asked.

Dottie nodded and smiled, her short blond braids waving. Dressed in worn jeans and faded blue knit shirt she was ready to ride shotgun for my regular Friday night shift.

"Two of those in a sack and a coffee for me," I said to the counter man.

"Half-pint, want a carton of milk with that?" he asked. She couldn't see the twinkle in his eye for the tall counter. She looked at me again.

"She likes chocolate," I said and took a sip from the Styrofoam cup. "Ow-w-w." I jerked the coffee cup away from my lips and spewed out the sip I had taken. "Are you trying to kill me?"

"I told you it was hot, Mack." He held an empty carafe, its insides caked with dried coffee.

"You didn't say it was scalding." I spit again. Dottie grabbed my arm and gave the man a disdainful look.

"It's ten o'clock and we're fixin' to close. You got the last of the coffee. Swing back by tomorrow for a free cup." He grinned and his huge belly jiggled as he slid a glass of water across the Formica counter. "Here, cool off."

I took a long swallow and felt the skin peel from the roof of my mouth. I slipped a five-dollar bill from my money clip and tossed it on the counter. "After that poison I may not be alive." I handed the sack to Dottie, grabbed the Styrofoam cup and headed toward the door.

The counter man laughed. "You love us here. You'll be back."

I set the cup on the top of my cab and looked around. A mist was forming. Rain wouldn't be far away. The shops along the street had long since closed and quiet prevailed, except for an occasional passing car. Atlanta was calling it quits for the night, except for the porn shops, sex movies, and prostitutes a couple of miles toward downtown. They didn't shut down until the last John stumbled away. The OPEN neon sign in the window of City Café went out. I could see the man and his wife through the windows stacking chairs on tables and mopping the coffee that I had just spit out. The streetlight thirty yards away cast gray shadows around my vehicle.

"Bur-r-. Hurry, Daddy. I'm cold." My angel stood on the other side of the taxi, watching with a happy smile and rubbing her arms to keep warm. Her hair formed a golden halo in the mist.

"I'm hurrying, Sweetie." I unlocked the car and we sat sipping our drinks and eating the divine cookies. My mouth was still sensitive and I blew on each sip. The sounds of the city were far away and faint.

I keyed the radio. "Cab 79. Ten-eight. I'm back."

"Ten-four, 79." The radio again was silent.

I finished the cookie and sat there sipping the strong coffee that I topped off from the bottle that I kept hidden in the glove compartment. Dottie looked away, pretending not to see. The counter man and his wife came out and locked the café door. He waved to us as they walked away.

"Daddy, why did that man call me Half-pint? He knows my name."

"Sweetie, he's a jokester. You are short, but you'll grow a foot this year. You won't be my GPS then. You'll be too tall to fold up on the floor when I have a fare."

"I'll shrink every Friday night, just to be with you."

"I wish." *Damn the divorce. I hope Deb will still let her be with me on weekends ...*

The heavy rain woke me with a sharp rat-a-tat on my cab roof. I looked down at the center of my universe still asleep, her head on my lap with that angelic look and her glasses skewed on her nose. I wondered if she was dreaming. *Is your old man included? Have your Mom and I soured you on marriage?*

As quickly as it came, the fall rain abated and left the gutter full and running over, the water glistening in the faint light. Even inside the cab the air smelled fresher, cleaner. I shook my head, stretched, and rubbed my eyes. Eleven-fifteen and no fares; slow night. I yawned and scratched my day-old beard. Dottie sat up, rubbed her eyes and laid her head against my shoulder. Got to stay awake. To relieve the monotony, I started the cab and pulled out onto Monroe Drive. Maybe we could see some action toward downtown. The wipers swished as they cleared the final rain from my windshield and the orange glow of the city brightened.

The radio came to life. "Base to Cab 79. Is this Mack-the-Knife?"

"Yeah. Yeah, Base. Ten-four. Where you been? I'm going to have to apply for food stamps."

"79. Ten-sixteen at 600 block of Blackland Road. That's in Buckhead."

"Ten-four, Base. I'm on it." I switched off the roof light, glanced in the rearview mirror and did a U-turn toward Roxboro.

Dottie smiled and showed me the GPS solution that she found. Ten minutes later I turned onto Blackland.

"Base, this is 79. I'm in the 600 block. Give me the rest."

"Ten-four, Cab 79. Go to 682."

We passed by large homes on this street, and most had imposing iron fences around the property. Five minutes later my headlights swept across the 682 address in a bronze plaque above the mailbox. The automatic gate swung open and I pulled into the long circular driveway. A two story mountain stone mansion with a three car garage on the side loomed in front of me, dark except for a single light at the front door. I stopped at the two four foot tall concrete lion statues guarding the entry. "Wow," Dottie said, "These people are rich." Without my reminding her, she folded up on the floor with the GPS, her head resting on the front seat.

The light beside the front door went out, and a woman stepped onto the porch. Mid-thirties, she carried herself with grace as she walked toward the cab; her bone-white face, almost radiant in the moonlight, framed by jet black hair. Call it intuition; I knew that I was in the presence of a real lady, a trophy wife. Bound to be genuine Atlanta aristocracy, not a despicable nouveau riche bitch; one of those who would look down their nose at me, and if I'm lucky get a five percent tip. The light wrap over her arm complemented her black sheath dress. She carried a small overnight bag, and I had seen enough third-world knockoffs to believe that her soft leather purse was a real Gucci.

I got out and opened the rear door for her. The faint aroma of her perfume met me as she nodded and sat down. She didn't smile, and the firm set of her jaw was betrayed by the tiny tear forming in her eye. I got in and flipped the meter arm up. "Where to, Ma'am?" I looked around at her. She was gazing toward the dark house. "Ma'am?"

Without turning, in a low controlled voice, she said, "Just start driving toward town."

I hesitated, but keyed the radio. "Base-79. Ten-sixteen to downtown." Dottie had a questioning look, and I winked at her. I turned onto Piedmont and then Peachtree Street toward the Heart of Dixie.

Ten minutes passed. I looked at the lady in my mirror. She gazed out the side window with a blank look as if she wasn't aware of where we were. I cleared my throat. "Have you had a good day, Ma'am?"

She looked at me in my rearview mirror. "I love my husband, but there are things in our lives that are hurtful. I just need to ..." She broke off. "Here. Turn left here on Ellis and pull in the drive."

I followed her directions and pulled in at the front door of The Empire Hotel. Very few people were in the brightly lit lobby. I looked at her and I knew she saw the question in my eyes. She nodded with a faint smile and opened the door. "Don't get out," she said and pushed a folded bill through the slot in the plexiglass partition, onto my front seat.

I was at a loss for words as I watched her enter the front revolving door. I got out and stood beside my cab for a better view. The tuxedoed concierge nodded as she passed and returned to his paper. She walked across the large lobby to the bank of elevators and disappeared. I got back in and looked at the $18.75 charge on my meter.

"Daddy, she gave you a fifty-dollar bill." Dottie had raised up and watched the lady walk across the lobby. I nodded and keyed the radio to tell the dispatcher I was clear. "Base. Cab 79, ten-twenty-four."

"Dottie, let's hope the lady is happy now." I sat back and held my breath that there were no little girl's innocent questions to answer. Maybe she was so sleepy that the possibilities just didn't compute.

Dottie yawned and crawled up onto the seat. She stretched out with her head on my lap, and I heard her slow relaxed breathing.

I pulled away from the hotel and cruised down a side street searching for some quiet place. Finally I found a respectable semi-dark side street and parked.

"Cab 79. Ten-sixteen at 250 Ellis, downtown."

I jerked my head up. "Ten-four, Base. I'm on it." I must have sounded groggy. I looked at my watch. It was 4:30.

"Ten-four, Cab 79. You awake? Pick up at side entrance of the hotel."

"Ten-four, Base." I turned onto the next street while my

mind scrambled to remember the night's previous activities. *That address is sure familiar.* Dottie hadn't moved on my lap. Still sound asleep.

Ten minutes later I pulled up even with The Empire Hotel and did a U-turn to the side entrance. I chuckled. *I knew that address was familiar.*

A man stepped from the vestibule and strode across the sidewalk. He opened my rear door and slid in. He was well-dressed for that time of night; suit and tie with monogrammed shirt. He laid his briefcase on the seat beside him. *Right handsome dude.* Slight gray showed at the temples through thick dark brown hair, and his Polo cologne permeated the cab. A smile played across his face as he looked straight ahead.

I engaged the meter and looked in the mirror. "Where to, sir?"

"Oh, home, I guess. That's 682 Blackland Road." I looked a him in the mirror. *You're kidding me.* I felt Dottie moving. *How long has she been awake?*

He turned pages in a Day-Timer and made some notes, then put the journal back in his briefcase. "Going to be a nice day," he said.

"Yeah. Good weather." I spoke in a soft voice, hoping not to wake Dottie, but I felt her move.

"May play some golf. Wife called. She went out of town to visit her sick mother. Just as well. I love her, but we're having our problems. I just had to have a little diversion." He managed a sly smile.

I pulled into his driveway and stopped at the front porch. The lions cast fierce shadows on all who approached. A twenty-dollar bill slid through slot.

"Keep the change." He got out and walked to the house.

Thanks a bunch. I watched him open the door and turn on the light. Dottie raised her head and saw him and the lions. She looked up at me with the hurt of a 20-year-old and then laid her head back on my lap. Her shoulders shook and I felt the wetness of her tears on my leg. I drove out and parked on the closest side street. She sat up and threw her arms around my neck. I held her and patted her shoulder. I felt her tiny heart flutter as she sobbed and clung to me. *She understands or thinks she does. Maybe better than I do. Very perceptive for a little girl.*

She sat back and wiped her eyes. "Daddy, did you know that Mom's got a boyfriend?"

I nodded. "I heard." *Is she comparing what she's just seen to Deb and me?* "Do you like him?"

She looked away. "I guess, but ..."

"But what?"

She hesitated. "He makes me uncomfortable."

"How, Sweetie?"

She looked down. "I don't like the way he looks at me."

I lifted her chin and looked in her misty eyes. "He hasn't ..."

I'll kill that s.o.b. if he lays a hand on her.

"No. No, Daddy. He hasn't touched me. I'd tell Mom and you."

"Promise?"

"Promise."

I looked at my watch. "It's almost time for you to go home."

"Do I have to?"

"Afraid so." I started the cab and drove as slowly as the law would allow. She clutched my free hand with both her small ones. We turned into our subdivision of small frame houses and pulled up in front of our home; Deb's after the divorce. The door opened, and Deb smiled and waved. Dottie walked to the door, and Deb knelt and talked to her. Dottie threw her arms around Deb's neck. I smiled and started the cab, then glanced toward my women. Dottie was running toward me, waving her arms. I rolled down the window.

Breathless and with tears in her eyes, she blurted, "Mom doesn't have a boyfriend any longer. She asked if you would have breakfast with us."

Ten a.m.: I sat in my cab outside City Café. Through the windows I saw the counter man and his morning crew working to be ready for opening time.

The neon OPEN sign flashed on. He looked out the window and saw me, then opened the door and waved for me to come in for that promised cup of fresh coffee.

Mister, you haven't got a meal to compare with the soul food that I've just enjoyed. I probably didn't eat ten bites off the table, but I squeezed the hands and stared into the sky-blue eyes of the woman that I love, despite our problems. We watched a noisy ten-year-old devour a stack of pancakes and then smile at us. The three-way hug and tears that we shed will last a lifetime.

I started the cab and waved to the counter man as I pulled into the morning traffic.

Grandmother Moon

Elijah David

Grandmother dozed beneath the watchful eye of the no-longer-quite-full moon. Her right hand held Perry's left, stretching his arm across the narrow aisle between the SUV's middle seats like a lifeline in the sea of memory.

Or forgetting, Perry thought. Perry had no illusions about Grandmother's ability to remember him or their relationship. She was past remembering, her mind swallowed up in a darkness as certain as that which surrounded the moon.

If I could draw the moon down in my hand, Perry thought, *I'd drop it in your head and it would shine into all the deep corners of your mind where our faces lie cobwebbed and moth-eaten. And you'd remember us again.*

But even as Perry stretched a hand to the sky, the futility of the act froze him. Moons did not leave the sky without fingers of gods hurling them down.

Perry's gaze shifted to the empty road before them, lit by the harsh yellow headlights of his father's SUV. His father had refused all offers to switch places, to let Perry drive awhile, despite the sleep that threatened to club them both over the head. The beams from the headlights stretched into the night like insubstantial fingers grasping for purchase in the dark.

Fingers . . .

Perry lowered the window, drawing nothing more than a

curious glance from his father, and stretched his arm into the October night. He did not look away from the road, did not let his sleep-numb left hand know what his right might be doing. The night seemed deeper as he pulled his arm back inside. But the car's interior grew moon-bright. Perry finally allowed himself to view the prize in his hand.

"Don't stare at that screen too much," his father stage-whispered from the front seat. Perry only nodded in response. Speaking any louder might startle Grandmother into one of her confused states. Perry had had enough of those; he didn't care to instigate another.

In his right palm lay a small pill the color and shape of the moon. It was not perfectly smooth nor uniformly grey, but cratered and splotched. His eyes turned back to the night sky, searching for confirmation that he hadn't lost it, wasn't dreaming. Where an almost-full moon had been guiding their way home, no moon hung in the sky. The stars shone more clearly. No clouds were in evidence.

Perry had stolen the moon.

At their next stop, Perry had to sort through Grandmother's medications and make certain she'd taken all the right pills at the right times. There were a surprising number of them, even if Grandmother was pressing ninety years old. The moon-pill still glowed in Perry's hand, but the fluorescent bulbs in the McDonald's parking lot diluted the moonlight. To most people, it was just another grayish-white pill, even if it did seem to shine a bit brighter.

For Perry, the difficult part wasn't slipping the new pill into the mix; it was keeping himself calm through the process, not giving away the fact that he'd just given Grandmother the moon to swallow like an aspirin.

Perry told himself his attentiveness to Grandmother as she swallowed each tiny cupful of medicine was only his due diligence. Old people sometimes faked taking their medication, didn't they? He was only ensuring she didn't miss any. Especially not the moon-pill.

The rest of the drive—all four hours of it—passed much the same as the previous four. Grandmother dozed. Perry's arm fell asleep. His father drove without diverting his attention from the road. Occasionally, Grandmother woke with a start from her nap and had to be reassured of the rightness of the world. The same questions had to be answered and reanswered and answered once again.

No, he wasn't her son. He was her grandson, Perry. They were going to Tennessee. Yes, they'd cleared it with the front office. And the Post Office. And the bank. No, that wasn't Perry's wife driving them. Yes, they'd checked beneath the mattress. (There was nothing there.)

As the night came round its axis and turned toward the morning—though not so far that the sun had actually rolled over in its bed—Grandmother woke again, but this time instead of asking where they were and where they were going, she gripped Perry's hand tighter than ever. She looked around the cabin of the SUV, and Perry swore that rather than reflecting the glow of the dashboard's LEDs, her eyes emitted their own ghostly light.

Then she locked eyes with Perry and said, "Perry. You're Perry, right?"

The lucidity of the question shut down Perry's ability to speak. He nodded.

"Perry," Grandmother repeated. "I haven't seen you since . . . it was a wedding, I think. Is that right?"

Perry nodded again.

"I have trouble remembering things sometimes," Grandmother continued. It was like they'd gone back a few years, back to when her mind had still mostly been there. Before the darkness had truly begun to take hold. "But I remember dancing with you."

They'd been the first couple on the dance floor after Perry's older brother, Todd, and his wife. They'd tried to be the last, but Grandmother's knees couldn't take that much movement all at once.

Grandmother's face screwed up with her effort to remember. The moonshine of her eyes blinked out, then reemerged as she asked the question Perry had been avoiding for the last day.

"Pop's dead, isn't he?" she asked.

For several seconds, Perry didn't have the words. His throat closed up and wouldn't let him speak the reality of why they were moving Grandmother. Then they came clawing out of his throat. "Yes. He is."

Grandmother sighed and turned away, though her hand still clutched his in a bronze grip. "I'd forgotten," she whispered before falling back into sleep.

The rest of that night blurred in Perry's memory, not unlike the night he'd viewed *2001: A Space Odyssey* under the influence of Benadryl. Only this time, his drug was sleeplessness.

Over the next few days, Grandmother's confusion—or

rather, her lack of confusion—startled Perry's father and the staff of the new care facility they had chosen for her.

"She's handling the change remarkably well for someone in her condition," one of the intake nurses said. "Usually a move like this agitates dementia patients."

They all said to take it as an unexpected blessing, and so Perry's father did. But Perry remembered the pitiful way Grandmother had said she'd forgotten about her husband's death, and he wondered if he'd really given her a blessing.

When they finally had Grandmother settled into her apartment, she sat reminiscing with Perry's father about events she hadn't recalled in years: Perry's birth, his father's promotion, deaths and marriages and birthdays and vacations from the last two decades that had all been thought lost to her forever. She didn't always have the details right, insisting on a blue dress when she wore green in the pictures, but wasn't that true even of people who didn't have dementia?

Every so often, Grandmother would look at Perry with that old glint in her eye. They had a secret, she and he, one that would do Perry's father no harm in the keeping.

At last, Perry excused himself from the room and sat in the hallway breathing deeply and slowly, refusing to let himself panic. Did Grandmother know about the moon-pill? Had its medicine—or its magic, Perry didn't care which at this point—worked so well that she actually remembered what—and more importantly, who—was responsible for her miraculous recovery?

But recovery was a strong word for a few days of clearmindedness. Better to wait and see.

That night Perry stared up at the sky, searching in vain for a moon he knew was not there. No one else seemed to notice its absence. No news reports of failing tides or animals acting unusually. No astronomers demanding to know how a rock that big could just vanish from the sky without a moment's warning.

As more nights passed with no sign of the moon, Perry began to consult moon charts, keeping careful track of the phases as they should be. Even he wasn't sure why at first. But then, on a visit to Grandmother, he understood why. The surge in her memory had been only that; she was fast returning to her demented state. She no longer remembered Perry's birth, or Perry's father for that matter. The lead nurse said Grandmother might be worse than before they had moved her.

Even through her forgetfulness, Grandmother still looked at Perry knowingly. Almost accusingly. None of the adults recognized it, but Perry did. He had worn that same look when his mother had died. Perry had glared at the doctors with every ounce of guilt-inducing shame he could muster.

And now Grandmother held Perry responsible for . . . what? Losing her memory? Regaining it? Regaining her mind only to lose it again?

Perry consulted his moon charts, seeking solace or perhaps understanding in their esoterically real pictograms. There it was. Tonight would have been a new moon. The sky would be black even if he hadn't pulled the moon down and given it to Grandmother.

And Grandmother's mind, so full of memories only two short weeks ago, was now a new mind, wiped clean by the very medicinal magic that had healed her in the first place.

Perry lay awake all night pondering how he could fix

Grandmother's problem. But he had only two options: leave her alone to swing in pendulum cycles from full to empty mind and back, or somehow draw the moon from her and replace it in the sky. But if he did that, never mind the how just yet, would she retain what little memory she'd had before the moon-pill? Or would she be left in the same phase as the moon she ejected? Worse, would she become a new moon permanently, no mind left to remember even who she was?

When sunrise finally came, Perry had decided. All he had to do was wait.

True to phase, Grandmother's mind waxed in the following days. She slowly returned to the small memories she'd had before that long moonlit drive. The nurses warned Perry's father not to put too much stock in this resurgence, but Perry knew by his father's smile when they visited Grandmother that their words fell on hard ground and took no root.

Perry bided his time. Grandmother's memories had to be just so when he retrieved the moon.

Then, on the night before the full moon, he visited Grandmother alone. His father was working late down at the church, preparing scenery for the Christmas play, and Perry knew he could visit without fear of interference.

When Grandmother saw that Perry was alone, she said, "It has to stop." It wasn't a question, nor a plea. Only an observation of reality.

Perry nodded, that same tightness returning to his throat to throttle the words before they could escape.

"What was it you gave me?" Grandmother asked. "It sits so heavy inside me."

The words stampeded out. "The moon, Grandmother. I pulled it down from the sky to light up the corners of your mind so you could remember us, and it worked, it really worked and then—" Guilt and sorrow choked his words out again.

Grandmother nodded. "And then it didn't." She took his hand, more gently than on the car ride, though she still held him like a lifeline. "So how do we fix it?"

"I don't know," Perry began.

"I don't think anyone *knows* anything in *this* situation, do you?" And she grinned at him, disarming his doubt. "But what are you thinking?"

Perry told her his plan. He hadn't done more than fiddle with the finer details since he first hatched it two weeks before. He couldn't allow himself to second guess what came next.

Grandmother considered Perry's ideas, her eyes shining with silver light. He wondered if she was thinking the moon's thoughts as well as her own.

When Grandmother decided, she did not speak. She stood and linked her arm with Perry's, still clutching his hand to keep from drifting away.

They stepped out into the well-lit garden, following paths of pale stones that should have been glowing in moonlight. A handful of other residents sat on benches scattered through the garden or walked slowly along in the company of attendants or relatives.

"I remember once you and Pop took me fishing by moonlight," Perry said, the words once again scraping out of his chest, his throat, his mouth, dying animals clawing for a last breath before the final plunge. "Everything—the sand, the wind, the waves—was cold. I never realized before that how different the beach was at night. The gulls were quiet, and the crabs scuttled across the dunes like ghosts. We didn't catch much, not like when Dad went mullet fishing with the cast net, but it was worth staying up late and getting salty again just to see the beach when everything was quiet and cold."

As he spoke, Perry's hands acted of their own accord. One reached up to Grandmother's temple, pushing back silver hair and pulling back something firm and much larger than a pill. The other held tightly to Grandmother's hand, not so much to prevent her from drifting away or keep her standing upright, but to keep him from losing his nerve.

Perry didn't look at his first hand, the one holding something larger than a baseball. But the garden path glowed with silver light as well as the unnightly yellow of the streetlights.

Grandmother gasped and said, "How pretty. Did you bring it for me, Perry?"

And Perry muttered that of course he had, but he had to put it back now and he reared back and threw the basketball-sized moon as far as he could manage. It wobbled in its course, and Perry's stomach dropped as he wondered if he'd failed altogether, but then the magic of gravity or the medicine of homecoming pulled the table-globe-sized moon up and into the midnight black sky.

"That moon sure is pretty," Grandmother said.

"Sure is," Perry replied.

There was a pause in which Perry sensed more than saw Grandmother look down at their hands anchoring one another in the night. "Who are you? Are you my beau?"

"No, Grandmother. Just a friend. Let's get you back to your room."

Perry prided himself on keeping the tears back until he'd seen her safely to her apartment and walked out to his car. He drove home in a mist of his own making, and all the while the moon watched over him, and every so often, he swore it gave him a knowing look. *See here, we have a secret from the world, you and I, and it's no harm to them in the keeping.*

Happy Mother's Day

Jerry Harwood

Just because I carry it well, doesn't mean it isn't heavy.

I saw my mother today. By chance. Not by intent.

I was in the store with my youngest daughter in the grocery cart. She was playing with a can of cream style corn and a box of instant rice.

My mother asked my daughter's name, and I told her. I gave her the formal "Lorena" rather than "Lori." There was power in that decision that I needed to convey, even if my mother didn't know I had made such a choice.

My mother moved her coat surreptitiously over her single grocery item, Miller High Life. I remember her joke. Every parent has that joke they say too often and think it is funnier than it is. "In dog beers, I've only had one!" She would laugh and laugh.

Her cart blocked my path. In my youth, I had to either turn and run or charge. Children don't get to choose their trauma. They can hide from it in a closet or tell it that it can't hurt them. But the scars prove otherwise.

Today I am not that trapped child. And my daughter, though in the cage of a shopping cart, will be freer than I ever was. A new me speaks.

"I got my five-year chip last week," I announced. I did not move the cart as I took the chip out of my pocket. My eyes instructed my mother not to come any closer, like that five-year chip was garlic or holy water to a vampire. I placed the chip back in my pocket, but now we both knew it could be brought out again.

I have survived much. One resident baby-daddy made me eat on the floor from a dog bowl when my mother announced her pregnancy with his child. My mother laughed and drank. In dog beers, she had maybe three that night.

Once my mother screamed and threw things. Her boyfriends played rough, first with her, then with me. That was the first time I took the white pills. My mother gave them to me.

I escaped by running away. But the rabbit hole I chased led me to many a mad hatter and Cheshire cats. Indeed, if I was Alice, then my mother was the Queen of Hearts.

But I am not Alice. Not all girls are made of sugar and spice and everything nice. Some are made of alcohol, sarcasm, and meanness. I am made of the same bolt of cloth as my mother.

I have felt her sorrows as I relived them in my own life. Unemployment. Abuse. Miscarriages. Broken Relationships. Homelessness. Sure, I chose whiskey and heroin over beer and pills. Window dressings but I lived in the same cottage.

I remember the day I realized I had run away from my mom to become just like her.

And at that moment, as my mind traverses the darker underbrush of my adolescence, I almost speak to my mother. I almost invited her over to see her granddaughter. I practically embrace not only her but all the memories of her trying to be a mom. The time she bought me a strawberry shortcake doll or let me decorate my brother's birthday cake.

A tenderness stirs inside me. Not all in her suffering was her doing. She too had a mother. She too had bruises and scars from a life she did not ask to live. I almost speak again. I almost tell Lori, "This is your grandmother."

Just because I carry it well, doesn't mean it isn't heavy.

I think my mother knew I was breaking. She takes a step toward my grocery cart. Can-corn Barbie and Rice-Box Ken were, after all, having an engagement party.

She does not know Lori, Lorena to her. She only knows my teen son. I see him tonight on visitation. His father's parents, who have custody, have allowed me that treasure. I know they worry more about his meal with me each week than they do him being out late on a Friday night with friends. They are right to worry. But they have seen my work. They know I have done what their son couldn't do.

I feel the five-year chip's comforting weight in my pocket. I recover my resolve.

I have fought. I have stopped listening to who I can't be, and allowed myself to be who I am.

My eyes remember. I do not recall the hardest part of my childhood. That would be like picking one grain of sand as your favorite part of the beach. I remembered that I learned to hold on until tomorrow — a combination of sheer stubbornness and self-love.

I always wear pants with pockets these days, and my fingers slip in my pocket and touch the sobriety chip. I felt the chip enter my bloodstream and speak to my soul.

The temptation passes, and I again see my mom's coat over her Miller High Life, the champagne of beers. In my mind, I picture my mom in her bedraggled state at a fine dinner party making a toast. I almost laugh at the image.

My mother never fit her skin. It was not just the physical brutality of drugs. Her soul wanted to shed her body and be somewhere else. Anywhere else. Any "Who-else." But she never had the strength to change.

As a teenager, she would disappear. Sometimes literally disappear, and I would play mother to my half-siblings. Sometimes her physical presence would be there sprawled out on a couch amongst her own wreckage and the debris. Those were the hardest times.

No, not everyone has a loving mother. But I love my mother. I know now I can love her without allowing in her toxicity. I can love without feeling bullied, without feeling worthless, without feeling responsible for her decisions.

For me, to learn to love meant leaving my sisters and brother. Those chains almost held me in the imprisonment of what is my family. I passionately loved them. I defended them. I attacked others who would dare devalue them. But the irony is I loved them and still didn't know what love was. I managed the trauma so we could live another day. And I defended my mother even when I knew there was no defense.

After all, if my mother was not a good woman, how was I to be of any value myself?

When I finally ran, I kept score of my value. Money never gave me value nor did relationships. Drugs didn't provide value, but they gave relief from its pursuit, at least temporarily. But they also taught me that I was unlovable.

I am not unlovable — a double negative. I am lovable. And being lovable may be the hardest thing for an addict to carry. It is a weighty truth.

My mind drew me back to the present standoff. My mother continued to stand, blocking the aisle. Corn-Barbie and Rice-Box Ken were now driving somewhere in a Capri-sun box. I think it was a Kiwi – Strawberry Ferrari. Or maybe a minivan.

"She is so pretty," my mother spoke. "She has my... your eyes."

Today I set out to:
- Clean my apartment
- Go by the thrift store, Lori needs some new shoes
- Give myself a pedicure
- Buy groceries for the week
- Make dinner and serve with cupcakes for Lori and my teenage son
- Read Lori a story before bedtime
- Not drink or use

There is flexibility. I want to get a nicer pair of shoes for Lori so I might wait till next payday. The grocery list didn't include a snackable, but it is her favorite. So, I will likely get her two or seven. I may or may not make the cupcakes.

There is also rigidity in my list. I will not drink or use. I will not place myself in an environment where such opportunities are readily available. My life will not venture into entropy.

I raised my arm to stop my mother's approach. As I did, the track marks on my wrist became exposed. Five years since the last, but the scars remain.

I don't trust anyone without scars. I don't trust people who aren't willing to be scarred for their commitments whether it be giving birth, jumping a ramp on a bicycle, or eating tacos.

My outward scars show many of my bad decisions. But they also show the birth of my daughter by C-Section, the weight I've added now that I am clean, and the general bruises and cuts from working an honest job in a factory.

My inward scars are much uglier. Some are callused, and some are still bleeding.

My mother would tell me my arms are ugly. Tell me I'm not beautiful, I'm not of value, I'm not enough.

I used to yell back that I was or tell her why she could never be loved either.

Or sometimes I would just run. Run and hide. Run, and self-loathe. Run, and self-hurt.

But today I just stand in the aisle surrounded by paper plates and bathroom cleaners. On my left are all things disposable and on my right the chemicals to remove the memory of an accident. I am neither. So here I stand. I can do no other.

This is the mom Lori will have. A mom with scars and a five-year chip. A mom who loves herself enough to get up the next day and live.

I am not that little girl I once was. I love my mother. But unconditional love means that you love even when you may not be loved back. She takes another step toward my outstretched hand. She wobbles a bit and is unsteady in her gate. Her breath is now close enough to be recognizable. The alcohol, the cigarettes, the years of poor hygiene, poor choices, and ruined aspirations.

Perhaps the woman I've always loved is still there and is fighting for control. Control to make a decision.

Corn-Barbie and Rice-Box Ken finish their adventure in their Capri-Sun minivan. I see now it is definitely a minivan, as Lori's hopes are tied up in being like her mother. I am proud of my minivan. And I'm proud of the work I did to purchase it.

I nudge my cart forward. My mother moves her cart to the side.

It is perhaps the kindest thing she has ever done. I am now free to go forward on my own terms. There are Snackables ahead and hopefully time to make cupcakes. I like the yellow ones with cream cheese icing. Lori loves sprinkles on them.

I move into the next aisle where the cereal is, and I feel a tear roll down my eye. Now that it is safe I hear myself whisper on this Sunday afternoon, "Happy mother's day mom. I love you."

A Lumberjack Thing

Riley C. Shannon

I am a freak magnet. I don't know how I do it, but I do it. Go figure, because I can't anymore.

I was on my way home the other day but there was a beat up truck blocking my street. It was pulled off to the side a bit and the driver motioned me past him. I figured I might be able to make it, so I started around him. I noticed the sign on his truck that said ETS Tree Service. I hit the power window button, zzzzzzzzzzzzzzzz down, and said to the driver, "How much to take down a tree?" He looked over his expensive-looking sunglasses and said, "Ninety-nine dollars to put it on the ground."

I said, "How much to clean it all up?"

He said, "Little bit more than that."

I said, "I'm around the corner and I've got a half dead tree I need down. Come around and look at it for me, gimme an estimate, okay?" He said he'd be there in just a minute.

I got home and had no sooner hung up my keys than the doorbell rang. I told Lu, my roommate, it was some tree guys and we met them at the door. It was a different guy than the first who was talking a thousand miles an hour.

"Whichtreeisit?"

I pointed it out (can these people not look up and see the

dead part? The thing is rotten! It also had duct tape wrapped around it because I got tired of telling the estimators which one it was. I'd just say, "It's the tree with the tape.") So, dude checks it out and says, "Four Hundred to take it down and clean it up." I'd had an estimate for $275.00, but that was a month ago, and I was on that guy's list. However, we had a severe storm about a week ago that dropped three healthy trees in the yard of the people in front of my parents' house; one on his pool, one on his son's truck, and one through his house. My half-dead sweet gum had survived those storms, but it was leaning, and some pretty big limbs were falling off of it with no help from wind or rain. It was also very close to the house. I told dude, "I don't know. I'm on one guy's list."

He said, "Lemme check with the boss man (the driver of the beat up truck I'd talked to before)." He came back and said, "Three fifty."

I said, "When you guys want to do this?"

Dude said, "Now." Well, ETS did stand for Emergency Tree Service, and they were there, and I had no idea when or even if that other guy would ever show up.

I said, "Do it." (Do you think that was impulse tree service buying on my part? Nah... I don't think so. I didn't want the dang tree through my house!)

Out of the truck stepped the boss man. He was a short, stocky guy, with dark, wavy hair, dark eyes, dark, tanned skin, with what looked like prison tattoos on his forearms. He was also wearing massive amounts (for a lumberjack) of gold and diamond rings, a heavy gold bracelet, and a heavy gold neck chain. He said, "Lemme draw up this contract for ya," and I knew when I heard him speak that he wasn't from around here.

He sounded like a New Yorker, or maybe he was from New Jersey. Either way, with all that gold, he had to be a member of the Lumberjack Mafia. And I was impressed.

His name was David and he talked just a bit slower than his cohort. He explained all this stuff and wrote the contract up. Then, he started yelling orders. I thought there were just two guys, but then two more appeared from the back of the truck. I hadn't seen them before. David said, "I've got a four thousand pound come-along and a two thousand pound rope. This one will be easy." Lu and I moved all the cars out of the driveway and set up our lawn chairs to watch the action.

I don't remember all the things he told his men to do, because he was talking pretty fast, barking orders, setting up. He pulled two huge chain saws from the back of his truck, and slapped a hard hat on his head. He set a ladder against the tree and sent one of his men up to rope it off. After getting the rope in place and the ladder down, he told his men, "Now, I don't want this thing to even brush the house. Watch the tension in the rope. She's gonna go down right across the back of the driveway and my concern is she's got two sisters at the top and I don't want it to split, so everybody watch it. I'm gonna notch it now." Then he fired up his chain saw and started cutting, as he put it, "Starting at nine and working around to six." As he cut, Lu and I watched the tree start to lean even farther. When he got half way through it, he stopped and yelled, "Check the tension on that rope!" His helper said, "I've got five feet left on it. She's good!" He started the chain saw up again and resumed cutting while his men tightened the tension on the come-along. As they tightened up on the rope, and he cut the tree, we started to hear the staccato popping and cracking sounds that a big tree makes when the tension on it is too much and the lean of the tree is too great. When it started sounding like firecrackers going off, the tree went down with a long WHUUUMP. The dead top of it shattered, the pieces skittering across the yard. Our lumberjack killed his chain saw and said, "That was a good one. Easy. I like those."

The guys cut the tree up and hauled the big pieces of brush down into the woods behind my house. As they worked, David took a break. I got them all some ice water and listened to them regale each other with stories of mistakes, near misses, broken bones, and general stories of logging mayhem.

David said, "That water hit the spot. You're a good woman."

I said, "Well, thank you. And you are a man after my own heart what with all those diamonds and that gold you've got there."

David pointed to the pinky ring on his left hand and said, "This one is for my successes." Pointing to the three diamond band on his left hand, he said, "This one is for my three daughters." Indicating the two rings on his right hand, he said, "These are for the hard roads I've been down in life." Touching the thick gold bracelet on his right wrist he said, "And this is for the ball and chain I'm married to." He paused for a moment and then pulled his shirt back to reveal the right side of his chest. "And this," he said, flipping the gold ring through his nipple, "is from when I got drunk one night and woke up with it the next morning. I *still* haven't figured that one out. Must be some lumberjack thing or something."

Lu and I both kind of grabbed at our chests and said, "OOOOWWWWW!!!"

So, my big tree is gone and no longer a threat to my house, I've got plenty of fire wood for winter, and I am REAL glad that David the Lumberjack didn't have something ELSE pierced, if you know what I mean...

Mama Oya

J. Smith Kirkland

1. Ordinary World

"I can hear their wings against the darkness," she whispered, "Paris, the angels are coming."

In her house at night I can almost hear their voices, too. They are like distant whispers between the drops of rain on the roof. But whether it was angels, thunder storms, hurricanes, swamp monsters, or any other thing from nightmares, I always felt safe in her house. Her name was Oya. The mailbox said Johnson, but most of us who knew her called her Mama Oya. I heard she had nine children, but I had only met one, my best friend Nevada.

I don't really remember meeting Nevada. We have lived next door to each other since we were born, both on the same day, February 2nd. My mother worked long days at the market, and I spent after school hours and most of the summer days at Mama Oya's. And when Mama Oya went on supply gathering trips, Nevada would stay at our house. It was like we both had two mothers, and we lived in a home with a slim alley between some of the rooms. The houses were so close that Nevada and I each had one of those old people grabber sticks, and we passed things back and forth to each other from our bedroom windows.

Nevada and I would go on great adventures in cardboard

boxes that became trains, spaceships, or submarines. We created fantastic tales filled with complex characters and winding plots. My mother loved them, and encouraged us to write them down. She taught us both to believe we could do anything we set our minds to. With the exception of a few bad machinations we had about making flying contraptions and testing them from the roof, she was always supportive of our ideas, and especially encouraged our imagination.

When we were eleven, Dakota moved into the house across the street. Nevada and I were working on our time machine, and trying to decide whether the plastic trash can or a tent made with an old blanket would be the best vehicle. Dakota asked what we were making, then exclaimed, "Wait right here," and in a few minutes returned with two big moving boxes and a battery operated red led digital alarm clock that no longer lit up all the lines, making some of the numbers look like alien writing.

"This will be perfect for the control panel. It's a little broken, but that might only make for some great unexpected adventures."

Nevada and I knew in that instance we had a new third best friend, and our adventurous duo became a trio. Paris, Nevada, and Dakota. We called ourselves 'The Misplaced Kids' since none of us had ever been to any of the places we were named after.

The Misplaced Kids were at Mama Oya's one evening planning what Nevada and I were going to do for our 13th birthday. We were going to be teenagers in just a few days. Dakota beat us to that milestone in November. We used to joke that being adopted was why Dakota was spoiled. A chosen and only child got a lot of love and attention. Dakota was born on November first, but Dakota's parents threw the best costume birthday/halloween combination party every year. And the 13th party, was the best yet. We didn't think we could top it. Besides, our birthday holiday, Groundhog Day, did not lend itself to a theme party. So we aimed to plot a big adventure, but we were running short on time.

2. Call To Adventure

A thunder storm roared in that day at noon and seemed to be stuck over the town. At any other place we might have been distracted from our adventure planning, but like I said, it always felt safe at Mama Oya's. But as evening turned to night, and the storm was still hovering, I noticed Mama Oya standing at the French doors that looked out into the courtyard behind our houses. She would pace back and forth between the doors and the window. It was like she was keeping guard, or watchout. Then she turned to us, and in the most serious voice I had ever heard her use, "Everyone down to the basement. Now!"

We had never known her to be afraid of a storm, so we obeyed without question or hesitation. She turned off all the lights upstairs and followed us down.

"Sit down," she said calmly and motioned us towards the basement couch and chairs. She looked back at the door, then kneeled in front of us.

"I can hear their wings against the darkness." she whispered, "Paris, the angels are coming."

"The angels?" Dakota questioned.

Some of our stories and adventures included fragments of the ones Mama Oya would tell us. Like the angels. I know people think of angels as messengers of God, or maybe even fallen angels. But the angels Mama Oya spoke about had nothing to do with either of those.

Dakota had heard enough of Mama Oya's stories to know this must be one of them, but Dakota had never heard Mama Oya talk about angels, and didn't believe that any of Mama Oya's characters and creatures were real.

"The angels," Mama Oya began, "are from another dimension. They slip into our world sometimes through holes in the sky. Most of the time they can be kept out by the lighting. But there are so many of them tonight. That's why the storm has been so intense and lasted so long."

"What do they want," I asked without need for any further explanation.

"They want Mother," Nevada said without doubt or emotion.

Dakota was beginning to be more scared of Mama Oya than the storm, but then had a realization.

"Oh, this is an adventure. Yeah, what do they want with Mama Oya?"

Mama Oya sat on the couch and took Dakota's hand.

"No, child, this is not an adventure. The angels are real. And they want my power. I have called the wind and the storms to protect us, but there are too many."

The thunder clapped so loudly outside that even in the basement we felt the vibration. Dakota was now officially terrified. I was starting to understand the things the people in town say about Mama Oya.

"Let her know when you're getting married if you want a pretty day for your wedding." "Ask Mama Oya if tomorrow is a good day for boating." Or on a windy day, "Mama Oya must be working on her potions." And Nevada obviously knew more about the angels and Mama Oya's power than I did. "What do we do, Mother?"

"I am going upstairs to hold them away. You will stay here until the storm stops. If I am not there when the storm ends, you will come find me."

Then she turned to Dakota, "You will get them there and back safely."

And finally me, "And you will save me." We all sat quietly as she gave us the final details before she went upstairs.

"The angels can't take me to their dimension. So they will imprison me somewhere here in ours while they try to figure out how to take my powers. They are weaker here, and they fear the lightening, but you will still need to find me as soon as you can."

"How will I find you?" "You are my child. Our love is a link that cannot be broken. Follow your intuition."

But that did not explain how I would save her from the dimensional monsters. As if she heard my thought, "You were born on the feast of Oya, just like Nevada. You are as special as one of my own. You know all the stories that you need. You will know what to do when the time comes."

The thunder crashed even louder. And Mama Oya started to go upstairs. "What about me," Dakota whispered.

Mama Oya walked back and kneeled again in front of

Dakota. When she again took Dakota's hand, Dakota flinched a little.

"Don't be scared. I know how strange all of this must feel to you, but you aren't here by mistake. You are Samedi's child. I am sure he sent you to me so I could protect you, and for you to keep my two adventurers safe."

With that, she went upstairs. We sat silently as the storm raged on for another hour at least. Then, calm.

3. Refusal Of The Call

We waited a few minutes after the silence fell before we looked at each other. We all stood at the same time and went up the stairs.

Nothing looked out of place. The storm was over. Everything was still. The French doors were open, and not even the slightest breeze came through them. There was no sign of the angels, or Mama Oya. Without speaking, we all moved slowly around the living room. I went to the kitchen. Nevada went to the bedrooms. Dakota went to the court yard. As if planned, we all met back in the living room, and stood there. Dakota was the first to speak.

"We have to call someone. The police." "And tell them what," Nevada replied calmly, "that Mother was taken by the angels?" "I don't know, but I don't know how I am supposed to keep you safe. I'm 13." I agreed, "And I don't know how I am supposed to save her. We should call someone. Some adult"

"No," Nevada said a little more firmly, "you heard her. We have to go find her. The only adult that we could go to for something like this is my Mother, and she has already told us what we are supposed to do."

I looked at Dakota, frightened, bewildered. Then it hit me. "There is another adult. Samedi, Dakota's father."

They both looked at me as if I had lost my mind. Dakota never had any idea who the birth parents were. But Nevada and I knew the stories of Samedi.

"If he is a real person, and he is Dakota's father, then we need to find him."

Nevada looked at Dakota, "Do you know the stories?"

By this point Dakota was numb. Angels and a father who was just some story time name until now. It was too much to process. Dakota simply said, "No."

"He is like Mama Oya," I started, "He can use the power around him. You know, to do things."

"Except instead of the wind and the storms," Nevada took over where I was hesitant to go, "his power is over death and the dead."

"My father is the Grim Reaper?"

Dakota was now more annoyed than shaken, "This is all insane. I love Mama Oya. I love her stories, but you are expecting me to believe that I am some sorta devil spawn."

"No. No," I tried to bring calm to the situation, "Baron Samedi is not a devil. He is a good man. He helps people. All of the stories are about him helping people."

"Yeah," Nevada jumped in, "if anyone in Mother's stories were my father, I would want it to be him."

Dakota looked away from us, "He's a Baron? So you really think this guy is real, and he could be my father?"

We waited until Dakota turned back around, and we both emphatically nodded 'yes.'

"Then how are we supposed to find him?" Nevada and I looked at each other, and in unison, "The cemetery."

4. Meeting The Mentor

Mama Oya said the Baron had a strong attachment to cigars, rum, black coffee, grilled peanuts, and bread. She said if someone offered him those as a gift, and asked in the right way, he would probably show up to help a person. We were not sure how to make coffee or that we had time to figure it out, but we found a bag of coffee beans in the kitchen and thought that would do. We also had grilled peanuts and bread.

Dakota said, "there are cigars in dad's den, and maybe rum."

We thought about it for a minute.

"None of us have ever stolen from our parents, or from anyone," Nevada said like a warning.

"Maybe saving Mama Oya is a good reason to make an exception," Dakota countered.

We all agreed it was.

Getting the rum and cigar was easier than any of us thought it would be. Dakota just went inside, passed without notice thanks to the television in the living room, took what was needed from the den, and came back outside. We all walked away from the house as nonchalantly as two 12 year olds and one 13 year old could. Once we were around the corner, we started running to the cemetery.

We found what we thought was the most respectful and cared for mausoleum, large columns, ornate bars on the windows, and it looked like the stone walls were recently cleaned. We placed our gifts at the door. Then stood there silent. Dakota finally spoke first.

"Now what? Do we say a poem or something?"

"I don't know," Nevada sighed, "I should have paid more attention to the Baron stories."

But I remembered what Mama Oya said once.

"She said, 'You offer someone a present, don't wait for a thank you. Just leave. Good things will come to you.' "

But it seemed like nothing was coming to us, good or bad. It suddenly felt like a waste of time. We should have been tracking down Mama Oya instead.

"We have to go find Mother," Nevada looked up at the sky, "I am supposed to know which way. I don't. I just keep thinking 'up'."

"Then up it is," Dakota said with confidence. "We can't exactly fly."

"No, but," Dakota pointed to the high ridge on the other side of town, "Trust your instinct, that's the only up from here."

We were about to leave the graveyard for the ridge, when a nasally but authoritative voice boomed from behind us.

"What are you kids doing here?"

We turned to see a tall, thin man standing close behind us. His eyes were hidden by dark glasses. He wore workman clothes that were old and dusty like he had been digging in the dirt. He could have been the caretaker, or a gravedigger, or a corpse. We all froze and stared at him.

"I said, 'What are you kids doing here?' You're not

performing some black magic shit are you? I don't allow for none of that."

"No sir," I immediately responded, "We don't do black magic. We were just leaving remembrances at the family tomb."

"Family tomb? That's your family tomb?" Dakota knew I had just made a mistake and took over.

"No sir, but we don't know where the Samedi family tomb is. We just picked a nice one to leave gifts for my father."

The man went silent. He studied Dakota like he was trying to decide if he was looking at a real person or not.

"You are a Samedi'?"

"That's what Mama Oya says"

Again the man said nothing while he looked Dakota up and down.

"Well, if Oya says a thing is true, then it's true."

And then turned to Nevada.

"And who is your mama, child?"

Before Nevada could answer, the man laughs, "Oh, I already know. Look at those eyes. They are just like hers."

He looks back and forth at Nevada and Dakota, "I should have known you two would find each other. My children always do."

"I am not your child," Dakota stated, again just as matter of fact, not defiantly.

"I would not be here if you weren't. Now, tell Papa Samedi why you need his help."

Dakota was not convinced. This man could be a grifter, but Nevada knew the moment the man spoke, this is Baron Samedi. And though Mama Oya had never said who Nevada's father was, and Nevada had never once asked, there was no doubt in Nevada's mind that Samedi spoke the truth.

5. Crossing The Threshold

"My mother was taken by the angels."

The Baron laughed, "If I were anyone else, I would think you meant she died."

Then his tone sombered.

"But I know what you're talking about. And if you're going to help her, there are some things I need to teach you quickly."

The Baron looked at me, "I know I didn't ask about you before."

I had to admit to myself that did hurt a little.

"How do you fit in this situation that my children find themselves in?"

"We're best friends."

"Well, then, you will be a friend of mine, too. But I know Oya must think you are special somehow."

"She said I was like one of her own. I have the same birthday as Nevada."

"Ah, she has told you stories of the wind then?"

I nodded. He shook his head sadly.

"But you just thought they were stories? Child, you start

remembering them all right now. You're gonna need them soon."

Then looking at Dakota, "And you, my doubting one, you have my eyes."

That was slightly amusing since we have never seen his eyes through the dark glasses.

"Oh not what they look like. What they can see, what they can do."

Dakota was not as trusting of the Baron as Nevada and I had so quickly become. The Baron took a step closer to Dakota.

"Look, I know this is a lot to take in all at once. You were just a happy kid being raised by caring parents, playing games with your friends, and then you suddenly look up and there are angels and some crazy old man telling you to call him Papa. I get it."

"It does feel like I should wake up soon," Dakota replied.

The Baron laughed a deep hearty laugh.

"My child, you are waking up now. And when this little adventure is over, and you are fully awake, life will be so much better than the dream you have been walking around in."

He took a coin from his pocket and hands it to Dakota. "You," the Baron said at me with authority, "give me a warm breeze."

I remembered Mama Oya saying when you need a warm breeze, just listen for it in the trees in the distance, and ask it to visit you. So I did. I listened till I heard it. In my head I spoke to it like it was a living thing. I heard it getting closer. And closer. And then I felt it on my face. I tried to hide the surprise from my face.

"Well done, best friend of my children. Now, I think you all have a ridge to climb."

Following Nevada's intuition, and the Baron's lessons, we were ready to begin looking for Mama Oya. As we walked out the gate, Nevada turned to the Baron, "You'll be here when we get back?"

"No. But you will see me again, child."

Nevada smiled.

6. Tests, Allies, Enemies

The most direct way to the ridge was straight through the downtown square. We were not talking a lot. I think we were all having internal dialogs with ourselves. I know I was.

"I can call the wind? Mama Oya thinks I am like her? How are we going to save her from beings from another dimension? We are just kids. I can call the wind? So cool. Other dimensions are real? No. well sure; it's science. Baron Samedi is real? Well, we met him. And he's Dakota's dad? I can call the wind?"

Yeah that one thought was the dominating one. My thoughts about the awesomeness of being able to call the wind were interrupted by Dakota saying something out loud. Something about seeing a cop.

"I'm going to tell him Mama Oya was kidnapped." And that snapped me back into the situation, "What?"

Nevada freaked out, "You can't do that! You tell anyone about the angels, and they think we are pranking them, or think we are high!"

The uniformed officer walked into the police station and

Dakota followed. We followed, begging and pleading for Dakota to reconsider. Nevada even grabbed Dakota's arm once as an attempt to stop the endeavor, and quickly regretted that with one glare from Dakota.

"Look, I know the two of you trust that Samedi guy, but for all I know he took Mama Oya and is leading us to some place where he can kidnap us, too."

"Somewhere like a spooky cemetery?"

Dakota didn't like that my logic made sense. If the Baron meant us any harm, he had the perfect opportunity at the cemetery.

"Ok. Fine. But you are 12 and I am 13, and the police are grown adults with guns."

Dakota went to the first cop in the building and told them Mama Oya was kidnapped. The officer took us to a room where two more officers asked our names, who our parents are, and listen to us tell them how Mama Oya was kidnapped after she told us there was someone outside, and for us to hide in the basement. We left out the part about the angels. They told us that they would help, but what they really meant was they didn't believe us and planned to keep us here until our parents came to get us.

Dakota looked at me, "Sorry. You were right."

"It's ok. But we have to get out of here. Hang on."

I could not hear the wind in the leaves from inside, but I listened for it anyway. It was faint at first. Then I realized it wasn't outside, it was in the room. There was a little yellow strip of paper hanging from the air vent. It as swaying slowly back and forth. I swear I heard the wind say, "I am always somewhere nearby."

I looked at the pile of papers on the officer's desk, and the blinds on the window, and the doors on either end of the room. The wind would have no problem making these move.

The uniformed officer broke my concentration, "The other two's mothers are on their way, but we can't locate Mrs. Johnson. I called child services."

That was all I needed to hear, time to see what the wind would do for me. Maybe I could knock the papers off of the detective's desk to make a distraction while we ran. The two doors blew open at once. They were pushed so hard that the glass busted out in one of them. The metal blinds rattled and swung violently making an unworldly scraping noise. The paper, not just one the detective's desk, but on all the desks flew up into the air and swirled around like flocks of chimney swifts at dusk.

I was a little impressed with myself. But could almost hear Mama Oya saying, "We can do nothing of ourselves, child. Always thank the ones who help you."

So I thanked the wind, the air conditioner, God, Mama Oya, my mother, everyone I could think of.

I saw Dakota's eyes motion both of us to head to the front door while rising slowly as to let us know to do the same. We all three were outside before the officers knew we had even moved. We took the first corner to get out of the line of sight of the station. Then we ran.

We had not gotten very far when a familiar voice yelled, "Paris, you stop this minute!" My mother. We ran to her, all talking at once.

"We have to save Mama Oya!"

"The angels have her!"

"We have to get to the top of the ridge!"

"We are the only ones who can save her!"

She herded us into an alley between some stores and told us to "hush" and "listen."

"Baron Samedi has already told me everything. And as much as I don't like any of this, I have always trusted him. If he says the three of you are the only ones who can save Mama Oya, then," she paused, "then I have to believe him."

She knows the Baron? She has 'always trusted him.' How long has she known him? What else does she know? What else has she not told me?

"Your bikes are behind the hardware store. I'm going to go see the police. I will be there quite a while to keep them there. I never saw you. You never saw me."

She tussled Nevada's hair and looked at Dakota, "Bring them all back safe." Then to me, "I love you." I echoed the words. With that, she left us, and we ran to the hardware store.

7. Approach To The Inmost Cave

The bikes were right where Mother said they would be. Mine and Nevada's had saddle satchels on the back, packed with flashlights and water and other things that we didn't have time to go through. We took off for the road into the ridges, into the woods.

At the end of the road was a parking lot for a trailhead that led to top of the highest ridge. We stopped there. Dakota and I looked at Nevada, waiting for instructions on what to do next. Nevada just stared into the woods. Dakota broke the silence.

"So, where does this trail go? Is there somewhere up there they could be keeping Mama Oya?"

"It just winds around to the top. There's an over look for the view," I began to explain.

"No," Nevada said sounding almost from a trance, "there is a side trail that goes to an old house."

I had forgotten about that. Mother took Nevada and me there on a hike once. Just once. She had taken us on lots of hikes around the area, but just once she took us to that old house. I looked at the trail, then back at Nevada,

"You think they have her there?"

"I'm sure of it."

Dakota and I did not question the response.

"Then that's where we go," I said.

"No, not yet," Dakota replied, "We have to have a plan first. What did your mother pack for us? Something tells me she knew what we might need."

I didn't doubt that either. Dakota and Nevada started looking through the satchels. But I stood there thinking. All our parents knew more than they have told us. They were placing a lot of trust in us to do something that seemed like way too much to expect from twelve year olds. I was thinking we should not be here in the woods, going to face monsters or whatever they were. I was doubting everything. Then Nevada vocalized my fear.

"What are we doing? This can't be real."

"Tell me about it," Dakota sighs, pulls out Samedi's coin and looks at it, "Angels, monsters, something take Mama Oya, this guy that's supposed to be my dad is some magician or whatever he is, and I have a coin with some weird language on it that must be for something."

Dakota holds the coin up to us, "what is this about?"

Nevada carefully takes the coin and studies it while he talks about the Baron.

"The Baron Samedi, Mother used to say, was much kinder than what he acted like. He could heal the sick from the edge of death. She said you would not die if he refused to dig your grave. She told lots of stories of the good things he did for people,"

Nevada handed the coin back, "but she never told one story about him and coins."

Nevada looked at me, "We're just twelve."

We both felt overwhelmed.

"I'm thirteen," Dakota said with a sudden burst of confidence, "and I'm really confused and scared, but there are grown-ups that think we can do this. And your moms have never done anything to make us not trust them."

Nevada and I nodded agreement.

"Now, she packed flashlights. She must have thought it would be dark before we get there. So, why would your mom have packed this broken alarm clock?"

I smiled, "because we are on an unexpected adventure."

We drank some of the water and ate the snickers that my mother packed. We each put a flashlight in a pocket, and started up the trail.

8. Ordeal

To get to the old house we had to leave the main trail. The side path was not very wide, and looked more like a deer trail at first, but it eventually widened and looked more like an old road. About half way to the house we passed an old cemetery with a big iron gated entry in a fence of metal bars. The gates were chained shut with heavy chains and an old rusted lock.

"I don't remember that from before," Nevada shivered as he looked at the cemetery.

"I do," I said.

I had forgotten about it. It didn't spook me at all, not when Mother had brought us here, and not at that moment. I remembered asking if we could go inside, but Mother said we didn't have time if we wanted to see the old house that day. Maybe another day. But we never came back.

"We don't have time to go there now," Dakota seemed to be channelling my mother. But it was true; we had to get to the house. But then what?

Nevada spoke my thought, "Then what?"

"We find Mama Oya. We make some distraction, and we sneak her out."

Dakota's plan sounded good. I told myself it sounded good. It was rather rough, no details, but it sounded good. At least until we got to the house. We saw a glow through the underbrush around the house. As we peeked through the leaves, we saw more of a shell than a house. Stone walls with holes that windows once filled. No roof. No doors. There was just Mama Oya sitting on the ground in the center, surrounded a dozen or more angels.

We had never seen the angels. I don't know what I expected, but it was not what we saw. They gleamed a yellow white light. They looked like people, with wings, just like all the pictures of angels you have ever seen, but they were not solid. They were made of light. And they stood, hands clasped in front of them, heads bowed. Their gleam formed a circle around Mama Oya, who sat cross legged on the floor with her head lowered too. She looked weak and fragile.

We were frozen. As we stood staring from the underbrush, I saw Mama Oya's back straighten, and her chin raise slightly. She knew we were there. I knew she did not look at us because she did not want to give us away to the angels.

I looked at Dakota and Nevada. Almost before they nodded in agreement, I could hear the wind rolling over the trees, and the sound of thunder as clouds gathered above us. The angels heard it, too. Their heads and eyes raised to the sky, and they screamed as the lightening flashed. The light from their gleam reached out of them towards the lightening. With each flash their gleaming weakened, and they looked like vessels of glass being emptied.

Mama Oya inched out of their circle and towards a collapsed part of the stone walls. Dakota and Nevada took the cue and went to help her into our hiding place. It all seemed to be working as we had somewhat planned. Until one of the angels noticed them at the wall. It reached out a hand towards them. An angel-like gleam was being pulled from Nevada's body. It snapped back when a flash in the sky pulled all the gleam from the angel, and the angel collapsed to the ground.

When we were all behind our hiding place, I called the wind to block us from the angels' view with a wall of wind and leaves. We had to get Mama Oya away from there. She already looked stronger.

"We need to be far away from here," Dakota took charge. But before we could move, Nevada's knees hit the ground, then the rest of the body followed.

9. Reward (Seizing The Sword)

"Nevada!"

Mama Oya rushed to Nevada.

"Nevada, talk to me."

No reply.

She looked at Dakota, "Help us."

Dakota's eyes widened, "How? What can I do?"

"You can heal!"

She took Dakota's hand and placed it on Nevada's chest.

"The light is weak, but it is still there. You can heal it."

Dakota looked in Mama Oya's eyes.

"I'm just a kid"

"No, you are young, but not just a kid. You are the child of the Baron Samedi. Somewhere inside you, you know what to do."

Dakota looked at Nevada, took a deep breath, and tried to look inside for that answer.

I realized the wall I had called was growing thin, and returned my concentration to strengthen it. It was when I heard

Nevada coughing as the air went back in that I turned to look at them again. They both had a gleaming like the angels but it quickly faded as Nevada sat up. Mama Oya embraced them both.

The reality of all of this was finally making its way into my brain. I could call the wind, the lightening. Dakota could heal people. We were not ordinary children. I wasn't sure what we were, but Mama Oya was. Her stories were all real, and this was not just a bunch of kids playing at adventures.

10. The Road Back

We hurried down the road back off the ridge as fast as Mama Oya could move. But she was still getting her strength back, and the storm I called was fading. It was nowhere near as powerful as what Mama Oya could bring. It weakened the Angels a little, but it was weakening me too. I was falling behind the others as we ran down the trail. I did not realize how far until suddenly, with a deafening sound of wings, angels were on the ground in front of me, separating me from the others.

I heard Mama Oya yell, "To me! Now!"

The angels directly in front of me emptied of their light and crumbled. Mama Oya stood gleaming on the other side of the opening left in the line of angels before me. I ran faster than I have ever run. I stood with Mama Oya and the other Misplaced Kids, as more and more angels were forming a circle around us. I called the wind, but the storm it brought was much less powerful than before. Mama Oya had used what little energy she had recovered to save me. I was certain we were not going to survive the attack.

11. Resurrection

Then Dakota yelled.

"Look!"

Pointing to the words wrought in metal over the gate of the old cemetery, then pulling the coin out, Dakota proclaimed, "That's the words on the coin!"

There are angels on the ground around all of us now.

Mama Oya grabbed Dakota's hand, "He was telling you that you have his gifts. You know now it's true. You can call an army to protect us."

"I don't understand!"

"His is the invisible realm of the dead. They are there when he calls. Just like Paris calls the wind, you can call your father's subjects. They will drive the angels back to their dimension."

Dakota, shaken with the realization from Mama Oya's words, stood numb for a moment. But returning quickly to the determined child we knew, and with a deep breath and hands extending towards the cemetery, screamed. It was a scream, but it reverberated like a musical note held for a long time. The angels took notice.

At first there is nothing. Then there are multitudes of dead rabbits and squirrels racing from the woods. It was like a horror movie where the poison apple turned Sleeping Beauty into the Queen of the Zombies. There were birds and raccoons trying to duplicate Dakota's scream. The angels were not impressed, and almost as if mocking Dakota, they turned back at us. They realize they had misjudged Dakota when the cemetery gates flung outward. The doors on crypts flew open. Slabs slid off the top of graves, and an army of skeletons and zombies rushed upon the angels, screaming with Dakota's voice.

Dakota's army began to draw the gleam from the angels, but the angels were still strong. I wasn't sure if my storm and Dakota's new gift could hold them back from Mama Oya. But the moon moved between clouds to illuminate the cemetery gate, and there stood a tall, thin figure wearing a top hat, black tail coat, and dark glasses.

"Well done my child," the nasally voice commanded over the screaming, "now let me teach you more."

He stretched out his arms and the skeletons and zombies became full flesh, clad in suits and dresses of black, white, and purple. It looked more like the people attending a fancy dress ball than a war with the angels, but the angels could not compete with the Baron's bizarre zombie force. They were pushed back away from us, retreating to the sky above us. The Mardi Gras clad dead followed them into the air.

Maya Oya stood in the road at the cemetery gate, "Paris! Nevada! To me! Now!" We ran to her. She took our hands, "Make a circle." I grabbed Nevada's hand. "Now call the storm. Call the lightening."

Nevada looked at her, "Me?" She smiled, "You are my child; aren't you?"

With that, the three of us called the wind to push to the angels back into the holes in the sky. The lightening tore through the dimensions. The thunder roared as the screaming subsided. I thought the wind would lift us up with the dead and the angels, but our feet stayed firmly on the ground. Then with one final clap of thunder, one last flash of light, it was all over. The angels were gone. So were the dead along with the Baron. Just the four of us standing in the moonlight through the leaves as the clouds dissipated.

12. Return With The Elixir

We stood there together silent for moments that seemed like forever. Mama Oya reached her arms out and pulled all of us together.

"I know you still don't believe or understand all that happened here. We will have a lot to talk about tomorrow. Right now, let's go home, my little heroes, let's go home."

With the sun set, and a dark road between us and our homes, we realized Dakota was the only one of us who didn't lose their flashlight somewhere along the way. We used that one survivor to light the road back.

We picked up our bikes at the parking lot, and pushed them as we walked along with Mama Oya. No one spoke the whole way back into town. As we turned onto the street where we lived, my mother was the first to spot us. She was sitting on the front porch, waiting. She jumped up and started running towards us. She screamed at Dakota's house, "They're back! They're back"

Dakota's parents came off of their porch and ran to meet us, too. There was lots of hugging and crying and 'I love you'.

I told my mother, "You won't believe any of this, but..."

She hugged all three of us at once, "I'm just so glad you are all safe. You can tell me all about it after you are all fed and rested. Maybe you can even write it down for me this time."

"I will." A promise I have kept now.

Before the Misplaced Kids went home with their parents that night, we stood for a minute just smiling at each other. We knew this was only the beginning; there were so many questions we would be asking our parents. What did they know about Baron Samedi? Is he really Dakota's and Nevada's dad? Is that why Dakota's family moved here? Did my mother know I could call the wind? Is that why we lived next to Mama Oya? Will the angels come back? What other monsters are out there? But for the moment, we were all just glad to be home. Dakota said the only thing left to say before we all went inside.

"That was a great adventure."

The Mover

Marcus Brian Bankstone

The phone rings. Tremayne Thompson sighs and mutters to himself, "It's probably another telemarketer." He actively became an introvert, ever since his abilities surfaced. The second ring reverberates through the house from the sleek black rotary desk phone, a gift from his mom when he first moved out. Of course he has other phones and rarely makes outgoing calls with the old beast, but it is tried and true while the newer models come and go. His answering machine begins to dutifully bellow out the caller ID digits. He thinks to himself, *Local area code, familiar prefix. I better get that!* He reaches across the kitchen table and picks up the handset of the rotary phone, the familiar feel of cool plastic resting in his hand as he pulls the receiver to his ear and settles into a simple wooden chair.

He answers the phone, "Hey, Jake! What's up?"

Jake replies, "Not much, Hadn't heard from you in a bit and wanted to see how you're doing."

Tremayne responds, "Yeah, sorry. Time does get by doesn't it? It's been what?" Pausing between each number as he thinks "three, six, four, four and half? Yeah, four to four and half months since we last talked. How are the wife and kids? Everything going well?"

Jake answers "Yeah, it's been about five months. Life is

good. Tommy's really liking football. They don't really win many games, but he has a lot of fun playing with his friends. You know how it is."

Tremayne simply replies, "Yeah."

Jake continues, "The coach pushes them to do their best and is also very supportive and understanding. They usually go out for some pizza or ice cream after a game." He briefly pauses. "Sarah has band recital tomorrow night at 8pm. Anyway, what are you up to?"

Tremayne replies, "I was just about to relax with some morning cereal and make my grocery list for later."

Jake retorts, "Morning cereal? It is nearly noon." and continues "Hey, if you're not busy tonight, Beth suggested I invite you out to dinner with the family. My treat. It is Tommy's birthday this Monday and we're taking him to Chuck E Cheese tonight. We'd love to have you. You know how the kids love their Uncle Tremayne."

He responds "While that sounds like fun Jake, I've been working a lot lately and am just going to relax and do some things around the house today."

Jake says "Ok, the offer still stands. Just call if you change your mind. I'll let you get back to your relaxing. Talk to you later."

Tremayne finishes the conversation with "Alright. Take care, Jake. And thanks for calling."

Tremayne pushes down one of the clear plastic cradle buttons to hang up and then lowers the receiver back on to the phone.

He thinks to himself, *I'll skip the Corn Flakes today. Sticks*

105

and Twigs will keep things moving. Sticks and Twigs is the nickname he gave All Bran original cereal. Cereal options are a little limited when using chocolate soy milk. As usual, the house is empty. So he thinks aloud.

"It was nice of Jake to call. I really should socialize a bit more often." *Who could I call?* "It's been a few months since I spoke with the Bobs."

He finishes his bowl of cereal and takes the bowl and spoon to the sink. There is a window just over the kitchen sink that provides a nice natural light to the room. He washes the dishes while glancing back and forth out the window and back to the dishes. Then he settles them in the bright yellow plastic dish dryer. Now finished with the dishes, he retrieves his cell phone from the bedroom and fires off a couple of text. One copy to each of the Bobs:

"It has been a while since I had some El Mason and relaxing chat with the Bobs. I will be there tomorrow at 7pm for dinner. Hope you can join."

Moments later, his phone plays a Star Trek TOS communicator sound indicating a text message. Bob2 responds:

"Looking forward to it."

Meanwhile, he wanders around the kitchen, flips through his phone and updates his grocery list. Thirty minutes later and Bob3 responds:

"I'll be there, not square."

Tremayne decides that he will visit the grocery store and collect his short list of items after his morning routine.

All cleaned up and ready for the day, Tremayne checks that he has all the important items before leaving, Cell phone, wallet, keys and pocket watch. He locks up and heads out to the Food City grocery in his light blue Chevy Volt. The short trip is largely uneventful apart from a squirrel crossing the street unexpectedly. He simply slows down abruptly to allow the scared and confused squirrel to change directions a couple of times before passing to the other side of the street. Inside the store he begins to gather items from his list. While on the canned aisle looking for some chili beans he hears a subtle clatter of a buggy and then senses two cans start to fall from near the top shelf. Acting fast, he reaches back with his left arm, spins around and snatches a can nearly frozen in midair just inches from the head of a toddler sitting in the buggy. The other can clatters against the woman's buggy and rolls along the floor.

"Oh Dear! Thank you!" the woman with the buggy exclaims. "I didn't even see it."

Tremayne smiles, nods and says, "It's okay. I'm just glad I was here to catch it," as he returns to selecting his chili beans.

It's 5:30pm the following day with an hour and half until dinner. Tremayne has been watching some TV and doing weekly laundry. He is confident that everything is in order and ready for him to leave for dinner. He hears a small growl from his stomach and figures getting there few minutes early won't hurt. Thinking, *I can enjoy some tea and chips until they arrive. I have my keys, wallet, cell phone, and my pocket watch.* He locks up, gets in his fully charged Volt and heads to town. Tremayne doesn't really like driving, but it is a necessary evil of living in the suburbs. There isn't any public transit out here except taxis or private online ride shares like Lyft.

Ever vigilante while driving, he is constantly scanning his

path for any possible trouble. A few minutes later and he is traveling south along the divided highway when a small pickup with a single occupant pulls out in front of a fully loaded semi-truck carrying refrigerators.

At this point everything feels like it is happening in slow motion as the truck driver swerves to miss the pickup and swerves back to maintain lane. Tremayne knows the truck is loaded. He had scanned it several times since he first saw it two minutes ago. He can feel that the truck is going to roll and crush the minivan in the turning lane and immediately scans the van, detecting a family of five. With his telekinetic mind, he instinctively flips a tiny switch hidden inside the pocket watch that is hanging around his neck. A weak but importantly fine tuned electromagnetic signal is now emitting from the hidden device. Tremayne Isaac Thompson feels an overwhelming surge of exhilaration, energy, and power, like a massive adrenaline shot.

The right tires of the semi-truck leave the ground. Tremayne exerts his power to push back against the several tons of metal and cargo, jolting the rig to the right, it settling back onto its wheels. Then he turns off the device hidden in his pocket watch and the signal stops.

With the crisis averted, the truck driver pulls over to gather his thoughts and Tremayne stops to check on him. He approaches the truck and states, "Hey, that was some fancy driving you did there."

The driver, looking a little pale, responds with "Yeah, that dude just pulled right out in front of me. I swerved but then I knew I'd messed up. I felt the rig going over. I don't know how it kept from rolling. It just kind of kicked back like a massive wind or something. I've never felt a wind THAT strong before."

Tremayne says, "Wow, um, you gonna be okay?"

"Yeah, I think so. I'm just going to check the load before I go anywhere. Um, thanks for stopping."

Then before walking away, Tremayne says, "No problem and good luck."

He walks back to his car and cautiously drives on to El Mason. He is thinks back to his daily practice and is thankful that he exercises his abilities in subtle ways. Tremayne still a little frazzled, realizes he is distracted and returns his focus to the road and world ahead of him.

Now safely parked and walking into the restaurant he allows his mind to wander a bit, trying to relax. Briefly thinks about how he usually does the dishes, the laundry, and makes the bed with his ability rather than with his hands. "How many?" a slightly mexican sounding attendant asks. Tremayne is snapped back to reality, grins and answers "Three amigos. Booth please." The attendant grabs three menus and leads him to a booth. Moments later a waiter brings some chips and salsa.

"Can I get you a drink while you decide your order?"

"Sweet tea, no lemon," Tremayne responds naturally, "Oh! And I'd like a shot of Jack please."

The waiter responds, "Yes sir, I'll get that for you. Anything else?"

"No, that's it for now. Thank you."

He doesn't normally drink. And certainly doesn't drink and drive. He thinks, *It'll be fine. Its just this one shot. We are about to eat. And we will be here for a few hours talking. I can always get a taxi later if I haven't been here at least two hours. What time is it?*

He pulls out and looks at the pocket watch, 6:28 and mumbles, "Looks like I've got some time to kill."

Then he grabs a chip, dips it in salsa and eats it. The waiter returns with the Tea and Jack.

"Are you ready to order!"

Tremayne thinks, *so far, service is fast tonight.*

"Not yet, thank you."

"Okay sir."

As the waiter walks away, Tremayne grabs the shot glass, gives the contents a gentle swirl, lightly sniffs it, then pours the entire contents into his mouth. It's a little quirk of his. He doesn't drink much or often. So, when he does, he prefers to savior the smell, taste, and feel. He holds the bourbon in his mouth, his tongue resting in it. It gives a gentle but smooth burn. He doesn't always feel the burn and sometimes it is smoother than other times. He slightly tilts his head back and swallows.

Settled in, he returns to his previous thoughts of how he practices his abilities. Washing dishes is easy enough, but more delicate movements require more practice. Like that tiny switch hidden inside the pocket watch. He practices with identical switches daily. Washing and drying of laundry is easy but the folding took a lot of practice to learn. And that can at the grocery store? Well, catching that was all him. Except, it was only possible because he can sense everything within a five foot radius at all times. And of course those vehicles were much farther than five feet. But he has practiced focused scanning. With his telekenesis he can sort of reach out and feel objects by pushing on them. It works as a sort of blind sight. A sight by touch. And of course it takes more effort to reach further distances and he can only reach about 1000 feet effectively without the aid of the device.

"Ready now sir!" he hears again from the waiter.

Over half of the chips and salsa are now gone. He had been absent mindedly snacking while lost in thought.

"Yes, Two more should be here in a min... There's one of them now. I'll have the enchiladas supremas."

Tremayne sees Jerry point his way and faintly hears him tell the attendant, "I'm with Bob." A small smile crosses Tremayne's face at Jerry's remark. Remembering long time inside joke of why the three of them call themselves the Bobs. Before Jerry can even take two steps towards him, Sammy walks in and says to Jerry, "Hey Bob!"

Jerry grins and replies, "He's back there."

As the two walk in together, Tremayne asks the waiter, "Can we get another set of chips and salsa please?"

"Yes, sir."

He remembers that Sammy drinks water, "And an ice water for one of the guys."

"Okay, sir."

Then the waiter wanders off to fill the order. Sammy and Jerry settle into the booth across from Tremayne.

Tremayne used to work with Sammy and Jerry as hyster drivers at a local packaging company called Pack'n Go. Tremayne casually starts the dinner conversation by saying, "I see you guys are still doing the Bob thing."

Sammy says, "Yeah, we still drop by Taco Bell together and use names like Bruce and Wayne or Clark and Kent."

Jerry adds, "Just wednesday we were Bill and Ted. It would have been nice to have you as Rufus."

"I'm just Bob these days," responds Tremayne. And continues, "I do miss the funny looks we got when using group names like that."

The waiter returns and takes their orders. Sammy gets a chicken sandwhich and Jerry decides on Nacho Supremos. The Bobs enjoy their meal and continue talking for several minutes about different topics such as Sammy's garden ideas and Jerry's battle bot challenges and design plans. Eventually, the conversation comes around to work when Sammy asks Tremayne. "Where is The Mover working these days? I hope you aren't letting your skills go to waste."

Jerry chimes in, "Yeah, we wouldn't want The Mover to lose his moves. You're legend at the company."

Tremayne tries to suppress a grin while answering his friends.

"I started a towing company. I figured that bigger is better. Rollbacks and tow trucks are bigger than the company hysters. Maybe you have heard of the company and its motto in radio commercials? Wreck Rolling, Never gonna give you up, Never gonna let you down."

A collective groan comes from Jerry and Sammy. Then Sammy asks the dreaded question for which Tremayne had been long prepared.

"If you don't mind me asking. Why did you leave anyway?"

His answer was technically true, yet incomplete.

"I knew that cameras were going to be installed. I understand and agree with why they were installed. Being able to watch the floor and understand how and why accidents happen. It helps management determine ways to keep people safe. I just don't like the idea of being watched all the time."

The more complete answer was that he didn't want to helplessly watch people get hurt. The cameras always watching and recording meant that he could no longer use his powers to protect his coworkers and prevent accidents without being discovered. Also, his work performance would have been affected. Much of his legend status stems from him being able to take turns and load faster and more easily than others. When he often made small mistakes that caused an unstable load he could just telekinetically compensate. More than once he had kept a coworker from being injured, crushed, or killed by falling boxes and hyster accidents. Sure, accidents had still happened. Just few were on his shift and never life threatening unless he was on the other side of the plant.

"You guys know I've always been shy to big brother things. Since you mentioned it. How has work been?"

The Bobs respond with a standard same old stuff, different day. The Bobs continued reminiscing about work, different incidents, and coworkers before saying their goodbyes.

On the drive home Tremayne is thinking about the people he has helped and feels that he should do more. Some of his thoughts are. *I could do more, I should do more. But I still need to stay safe. It is dangerous to me, my family, my friends and anyone I know if my abilities are discovered. Like a superhero, I will need to keep my identity a secret. I'll need a costume and a name. No capes or lose bits. Those things are dangerous. Probably should have a full face mask to hide my face and hair. I guess I could wear a wig and prosthetic mask. But that is really just too complicated. I can start with something simple. Like a green screen body suit. What name can I use?* Several moments pass between each name; Sometimes a few seconds, sometimes a few minutes.

Hover Brother, Bouyancy Bro? No, those are bad ideas. Kenetisys. Maybe the name shouldn't reflect my only real power. First impression will likely be of me flying or apparent super strength. They don't have to know that it is by telekinesis. Wonder boy? Nah, I don't want to be referred to as a kid, child or boy. I could do an acronym for a name. Or maybe a name to reflect positive ideals, like a guardian or protector. Tremayne pulls into his driveway, and disables his home security.

Treymayne happily begins to settle in and relax from his eventful day. Still pondering name ideas, he sits at his computer and uses the internet to search synonyms and other language translations for words like guardian, protector, protection, and sentry. After a few hours he gives up for the day and prepares for bed. The pocket watch device is responding to the polling from his computer and cell phone. All the home motion detectors, outside cameras, and other security sensors report as functioning properly. He places the watch on a wireless charger on the bedside table. The last thing he does before going to sleep is to telekinetically push a tiny button inside the watch device that will emit a different signal. When he does, his world will go numb. This signal greatly weakens his abilities. Tremayne built the device for this very reason. Accidental use of his powers while sleeping, like sleep walking, could reveal his abilities or worse hurt others.

Tremayne does one more scan, lays back and telekinetically flips the light switch across the bedroom to turn off the lights. Then he pushes the tiny button and closes his eyes. As he drifts off towards sleep he decides on a name. **FlipSwitch!**

The Mover is an introductory chapter or episode of the planned stories of FlipSwitch by Marcus Brian Bankstone.

Share Taxi

Jerry Harwood

1

Faustin jerked awake in his chair and instinctively swatted at his arm. In the dim light from his single desk lamp he saw a cockroach hit the ground. It bounced on impact and then landed on its back. The creature's legs were desperately writhing as it sought traction.Faustin looked around and realized he and the cockroach were alone in the third floor office. Behind on his notary work, he had stayed after hours. What used to be a rubber stamp if someone had paid their fees was now a political nightmare. He was required to sift out any Tutsi papers that might have made it into the que before April 7th.

He couldn't recall when he fell asleep but apparently it was on one Ntakirumana family. He stacked his papers neatly and placed them in the wired "incoming" box carefully. The precarious mound was higher than the mesh sides of the basket and threatened to topple at any moment. As he rose from the desk Faustin wiped his eyes getting the sleep, that is what his mother always called it, out of the corners. Removing the palm of his hands Faustin blinked a time or two trying to convince himself to wake up for the trip home. It was then he again looked at the cockroach.

Faustin raised his foot over the bug and paused. The office

mores was to kill them on sight. Some coworkers even made sport of the tiny carcasses. The place was infested. However, this particular one had the distinction of waking him up. Realizing he might have woken to the jeers of his office mates in the morning Faustin's worn sole now towering over the impotent bug held its position. Then, as if given an officially sanctioned reprieve, his boot averted to the side where he gave it a gentle nudge. The bug slid across floor but remained upside down. e again nudged it with his boot. This time the bug tumbled, found purchase, and was gone.

"Ungrateful pest," Faustin uttered with a smile threatening to overtake him.

2

Taking his coat and briefcase he walked down the stairs and in to the streets of Kigali. It was dark, perhaps close to midnight. Twegeranes, roughly translated as "share taxis," would not be plentiful this time of night. Faustin knew hopping the two he normally used would take several hours or more since they often waited till their passenger seats were nearly full before departing their station. Instead, he got in the que for one that ran slightly north of his home. It did not require exchanging taxis and he could walk downhill through the woods the half mile or so after drop off. There was actually a well-marked trail where some of his neighbors trod the path daily.

A few minutes later a Toyota minibus with "Muzic Pleze" written on the side and music notes decorating the otherwise brown exterior pulled off the road into the loading lane. Stepping in to the share taxi Faustin paid his fare and found a seat on the third row. Right before they departed a woman and her young daughter scurried on to the bus from a nearby building's alley. She was hunched as she ran and Faustin thought if she stood straight she would likely be a head taller than himself. Likely she had Tutsi blood on her mother's side. Her father must be a registered Hutu for her to be out in public. Although the lateness of the evening suggested her story might be complex. As she and her daughter stepped in to the share taxi Faustin committed in his mind not to ask. She headed for the third row and placed her daughter on top of Faustin's briefcase, positioned like a ready-made high chair on his lap. She gave him a short smile that asked if this was acceptable. Faustin smiled back agreeing to the nonverbal contract without speaking. The woman edged her bottom on to what little seat remained in the row. She placed a finger over her lips instructing her daughter to remain silent. The girl obliged.

A man in the row ahead turned to look the woman up and down with longing eyes that perhaps hovered their insatiable gaze a bit too long in certain places. "It is late for such a pretty lady to be out. Not safe. Lots of soldiers and others out that would take advantage of you these days."

He smiled a smile that was half kindness and half threat. The woman looked down not making eye contact. She did not respond and the man turned back to the front of the share taxi. The silence set the tone for the ride.

The share taxi drove a mile or so and then pulled off to pick up additional passengers. Per courtesy passengers exiting did so expediently before new passengers entered. Then the share taxi returned to the road. Then another stop, and then a third. On the third one person exited and a couple entered. As they were finding seats the woman seized her daughter and stepped fervently out of the Toyota. Faustin watched as the two again hunched over made their way into the shadows. All watched but none spoke. Talk entangled. These were dangerous days as Hutu soldiers continued the war against Tutsi rebels.

3

Faustin had taken this trail to his apartment before and had even done so at night.But the killings had changed the landscape. Several heavy trucks had been through and had torn asunder the bushes and trees he previously used as familiar guideposts. The trail itself seemed unclear and trodden over. He worried he was becoming lost, maybe even to the point of not being able to retrace his path. Relying on the fact that the entire journey was downhill, he continued on what most resembled a true path forward. Faustin was deep in his own thoughts trying to remember his path when he was startled. Awakened again to his surroundings he became motionless.

"Help!" There was a sobbing that punctuated the cry. "Help! Sir! Help!"

Faustin dropped his briefcase and extended his hand to a nearby tree as his legs began to buckle. There was no light and no visible silhouettes.The voice was muffled and the tears more so than the words pierced the night's canopy of silence.

"Stay silent. Please. Talk entangles," Faustin thought.

"Help!" came the tearful voice.

Before he made a decision in his mind, Faustin's body moved right, toward the sound. A cautious, meticulous two minute walk later his nostrils felt the first attack on their senses. An odious stench of human feces and rot permeated around him like an invisible fence preventing anyone from coming inside what he began to see as a clearing.

"Is someone there? Help!" The sobs again punctuated the plea, this time growing in boldness as the voice sensed someone had approached.

Squinting his eyes, Faustin still could not see anyone in the clearing. Step by cautious step he exited the protection of the wood's canopy. Scanning ahead he almost missed the pit. It was the new wave of rot and death, this time he was certain it was death, that caused him to stop before entering the chasm himself. It was at least three share taxi's deep and four wide. The stench pummeled Faustin, pushing him back a step into a fallen tree branch. The branch snapped.

"Hello? Hello? Help!! Help me please! I'm still alive! Please!"

Clarity. A killing field. Tutsi's set in a common grave.

Faustin turned and began moving as quickly as he could out of the clearing and back to the woods, back to his previous path. This time with a reckless haste he felt a thorn bush catch his shirt and reach flesh. Continuing forward Faustin felt the thorns dig deeper before their final release of their hostage. Panting he looked back at the clearing, the place Tutsi bodies were impounded, where the voice began again to sob. He fell to his knees and recognized he was by his briefcase. As he rose Faustin determined to turn back and make his descent to his apartment. Then a very faint cry reached him, "Please. If not me then my baby."

4

Faustin put a swath of his handkerchief on his laceration and then a piece of tape to hold the makeshift bandage. Then he washed the blood as best he could from his shirt and pants. He would patch the shirt tomorrow, but would never be able to wear it to work again. Right now he needed to sleep. He laid in his bed not even bothering climb under his sheet. His eyes closed and he slept. He slept and his only dream was of that cockroach returning to his family in the wall, telling them of his near peril.

5

Exiting his normal share taxi the next morning he saw Hutu soldiers on the taxi lane where passengers loaded. They were pulling everyone off the share taxi that followed his route the evening before. Faustin thought he saw the man who had spoken to the woman on the bus but averted his gaze before the man might recognize him in return. Walking toward his office, Faustin heard them asking about a Tutsi woman and her daughter. One officer was yelling at the driver who was trying to explain he was not working the night before. These were dangerous days.

6

At lunch Faustin realized he had not packed a sandwich in his briefcase. Hungry, he rose from his desk and left for the grocery shop on the bottom floor. He set some crackers and hard cheese in a basket along with a pad of butter and a bread roll. He would keep what he did not eat at his desk and carry what remained home in his briefcase. There was a subtle whisper in the back of his mind that he was buying too much food for another reason but Faustin ignored the mental muttering. Paying for the basket and a water he stepped out on the front stoop where he saw Jean-Bosco eating. Faustin sat near his officemate and opened his package of crackers. As he pulled the cheese out of his bag he realized he had no way of cutting it or spreading the pad of butter. Jean-Bosco saw Faustin's face fall and extended his knife handle first.

"Here you go."

"Thank you."

"Looks like you had a rough night? Staying late again?"

"Yes," Faustin replied.

"So much to do."

Faustin was thankful his habit of staying over was an assumed reason for his current lethargy.

Jean-Bosco nodded and then looked to Faustin's market bag, "Forget your lunch?"

Another assumption as Faustin always brought a lunch. "Yes. And you?"

"No. Rode the share taxi this morning. Soldiers dumped my lunch out. Said they were looking for a Tutsi woman and a kid. Not sure if they thought I was hiding her in my lunch bag," Jean-Bosco chuckled, "but you know… you can't argue."

"These are dangerous days," Faustin replied.

"Yes they are. I figure if that lady made it out of town she is gone. You know lots of those people are scurrying across the borders or hiding in the crawl spaces of people's homes."

"Like cockroaches," Faustin thought. He had heard the term used by soldiers describing the Tutsis. He nodded to Jean-Bosco. "Dangerous days."

7

Looking at the ever-growing stack in front of him Faustin recognized he had spent six hours and was still working on the same two documents. His outgoing box, normally full, had one and only one document ready. He knew staying over would not render any better results so he prepped to leave. He closed his brief case after confirming the extra food was there. Perhaps he should just leave it on his desk rather than carry it back and forth? No, best to keep it with him. A few work papers he knew he wouldn't do anything with were put in and the briefcase was shut without further rumination.

Exiting, Faustin walked by several empty desks. Reflecting on Jean-Bosco's "those people," Faustin thought about the staff members, co-workers, friends who were gone and their desks remained with their last day of unfinished work a memorial. "Those people" had been just "people" a month ago. Before the assassination, before the killings, before the dangerous days. "Those people." Those not already dead were running. Where too Faustin could only imagine.

Faustin's mind continued to spin. He hardly recognized it when he passed his share taxi loading area and returned to the area he had taken the night before. The one that would lead him to a walk through the woods.

8

Faustin exited the share taxi and stopped by a nearby food cart. These peddlers were one of the few groups who seem to have not been affected at all by the last few days. He picked up some cookies and drank a coke. He drank slowly, watching the few others who might venture through the woodland path. Once satisfied he would not find himself with unwanted accompaniment on the trail, he returned the glass coke bottle to the vendor and purchases a one liter water to take with him.

An odd thought crossed his mind that this purchase, not the other small decisions made this afternoon, sealed his decision. The food perhaps was simple leftovers, the different share taxi a whim, but the water was intent. Faustin entered the trailhead. A bit earlier in the evening than yesterday, he was able to recognize the tracks of the heavy machinery that had excavated the hastily formed burial hollows. Faustin could see today how they differentiated from the footpath. Coming to the primary path of the machinery, he stepped off the path toward the pits.

The smell again browbeat his senses. It was almost enough for him to turn and go back home. These were after all, dangerous days. The smart thing was to keep to yourself and not be involved with "those people." "those people..." "people..."

Approaching the pit's edge he lowered himself to his stomach. He took his handkerchief out of his pocket and covered his mouth as he scrutinized the hole. It was dark. The light was dimmer for evening now approached but there was a different kind of dark here as well. A dark made from rampant of death and decay. A dark made from the feral wickedness that crafted this place.

"Hello?" Faustin spoke quietly. Almost as if not to be heard. "Anyone in there?"

9

Her name was Uwimana. She and her newborn son had been there four days. She ran out of breast milk yesterday and her son had stopped whimpering. She had spent her day placing her ear near his mouth to feel his breath in fear his spirit would leave. She drank the water in sips, ate, and cried. Faustin asked a few questions but all he received were her waterless tears and her *murakoze*, her thank you.

10

The next morning he left early. He carried his pantry's food and two one liter bottles in his briefcase. The trip was much more arduous up hill. Faustin stopped twice to catch his breath and also to make sure he was alone. Reaching the pathway of the heavy equipment he turned to traverse the flatter ground and caught speed. As he crested the small rise, manmade by the large backhoes that had dug these killing fields, he heard himself say with winded breath, "Uwimana! Uwiman…"

About to speak again he dropped his briefcase and placed his hand over his mouth. Near the edge of the pit were two Hutu workers. "If they didn't hear you yelling they will surely have seen you. Stupid. Stupid. Stupid. Faustin.You know better."

What he did not say was, "What are you even doing here."

Faustin collected his fallen briefcase noting that the bottom edge was damp. "Dang. One of the bottles must be leaking." He stepped in to the woods and down the rise. In his haste he felt the makeshift bandage fall from his skin under the shirt. A swift glance confirmed the wound was again bleeding. He untucked the shirt and wiped the new flow with his finger. A new flow began before he could resolve the red stain upon his current finger. It was not a harmful cut. It was not deep, but it would ruin the shirt.

Thinking again of the two soldiers, Faustin lowered himself to the ground behind a fallen tree. Opening the briefcase he saw his few work papers were wet. The bottles were full but one top had come loose. He did his best to fasten the top securely and re-latched the briefcase.

Now to wait. And to hope. Hope they did not see him. Hope Uwimana and the baby are ok. Hope the workers leave. Hope his absence at work will go unnoticed. Hope whatever he was feeling, this belief that somehow he has to help, is meant to help, isn't a mistake. These are indeed dangerous days.

11

The backfire of the old Suzuki Jimmy jeep was at the same time terrifying and celebration. A few seconds later he heard the tires drive down the path he had recently trekked. Faustin's mouth tasted the dust cloud as it settled in the Jimmy's wake. Cautiously, Faustin rose from his position and saw the pit was clear of people.

This time with greater caution he approached the opening, "Uwimana?"

"Oh *murakoze. Murakoze.* I had thought you were in trouble when I heard your voice and then those men…"

Her voice faded into silence but the fact resonated that she knew his voice, was listening for his voice. He could not remember his voice ever mattering to someone before. A smile crossed his face and he realized it had been a long time, perhaps weeks, since he had felt those muscles stretch.

"I brought you some water and food. I'm sorry, it was only what I had in my home. I am a bachelor." Faustin lowered the bottles as far as his hand would reach then let go for them to drop to Uwimana. Then he did the same with the food.

"Please, help me out of here. I'm down here with so much… so much…."

"…death" is what Faustin knew she wanted to say. But he also knew she was on a razor's edge of sanity. Standing on corpses in a dark crater holding an infant was already too much to bear. The sentence ended without its final word being vocalized.

Of course, in all his planning to bring her food he had not thought about her greatest need to escape. She must think him a fool. He looked up for anything to reach to her. A branch from a felled tree? Maybe some line left behind by the workers?

"Help us out," she pleaded again.

"I did not bring rope," he reluctantly admitted. "Wait."

Faustin's scanning of his surrounding became frantic. Nothing looked usable. Maybe he could ask her to search below? No, he couldn't ask her to move through a sea of men and women, neighbors and friends maybe. She needed to be out of there, not immersing herself in that darkness. Then he saw it. A piece of vine sat a few meters off the clearing.

The vine was just long enough to reach her. Somehow extending it and seeing her touch its end gave him a sensation. It was forever to be in his mind the first time they held hands. But the moment was short-lived. Her tears brought him back to focus.

"I can't. My shoulder."

For the first time he noticed her right arm was covered in a brownish red that did not match the light green color of her blouse. Blood. Her blood. Her arm lay limp against her body. Why had he not noticed before? It was dark. He was scared. He was… a notion passed his mind that just didn't fit the situation. Culpably, he didn't notice because he was too busy being besotted with this woman he had never even truly met. He was too busy being drawn to her.

"Can you grab it with the other arm?"

"Not and hold my child while I climb."

And there it was. They could not both escape. Not in this manner.

"Umimana, do you trust me?"

"Yes," she paused, "You are kind. I do."

"I will have to leave and come back."

A moment of silence. Then another. Palpable hesitation. Finally, "Ok. Please. Hurry? I'm scared. Those men. My baby. If they hear him cry. Please. Hurry."

As Faustin opened his mouth he searched for what to say. What words could help her have confidence? What could he say to take her fear? Oh what he would give to provide her the feeling of being safe. To even switch places with her. His freedom for hers. His mouth opened, the odor of the pit again assaulted him, and he closed his lips without responding. Resolutely he turned and began his trip.

12

Instead of moving up the hillside to the bus stop he went again to his apartment. He would be late either way. This way he would have just overslept but be freshly showered and have a new shirt. He showered quickly and dressed. Then he exited his apartment to the loading area, really no more than a long dirt emergency lane, for the share taxis. He thought for a moment of abandoning work altogether, buying the rope, and returning. But the shower had sobered his thinking. There would be too many questions. And where to buy rope? If soldiers saw him? Where would he take her? Not to his home in daylight. He remembered the mom and her daughter. It must be at night under cover of darkness. He would go to work. At close he would leave, find the rope, and go back at night.

The share taxi was lightly occupied and as he pulled in to work. Faustin realized it was nearing lunchtime. Maybe he could avoid walking in to questions if he could get to his desk while most were at lunch. Cautiously, he entered the floor room where the multitude of desks were arranged. No pattern but rather a hodgepodge of old office furniture, miscellaneous desk chairs, and an assortment of filing cabinets filled the space. He made his way to his desk and took his seat without the few people working through lunch making comment. His chair with its missing wheel teetered as he placed the wooden block under the foot where a wheel should have been.

Then Mr. Kayumba, his supervisor, approached.

"Working through lunch Faustin?"

Does he know? Is this a test? Ben Kayumba had never been anything but kind to Faustin since he began as manager a few years before.

"No sir. I did not make it in on time this morning. I will not take lunch and will stay late."

"Not too late,"

Ben placed a kind hand on Faustin's shoulder, "We have much work but it is not good to be out these days late. I hear several share taxis have even stopped running at night."

"These are dangerous days," Faustin replied.

"Yes indeed," Ben replied. "Yes indeed."

And with that Faustin was left to his work. A few nearby employees spoke as they returned but all seemed satisfied that he simply slept in and arrived late. Then Jean-Bosco entered the room. His conversation from yesterday serving as permission to speak. Talking entangles.

"That does not seem like your character to be late Faustin?" Jean-Bosco had remarked. "Soldiers again?"

"No. Today I simply overslept."

"Well you still look tired my friend. If I didn't know you I would think you were out at a singles bar!" He placed his hand on Faustin's back patting him twice. Then he too continued to his desk. It would be the last time Faustin would ever speak to him.

13

Before close Faustin went to the storage closet under pretext of obtaining a broom to sweep his area. There he saw nothing that would do for rope. He closed the door and returned to his desk with the broom, made a few token strokes around his desk, and returned the broom. He had barely done any work for the second day in a row. His mind and heart were elsewhere. Was she ok? The baby? Did the men return? Where could he find rope? Should he ask someone to help him? His mind was a whirlwind and his emotions a rollercoaster. Work had to be set aside so he could keep his composure of stoicism.

Hours ticked by excruciatingly. Finally, after all had departed and darkness had fallen, he prepared to leave. Faustin gave a modicum of attention to stack the papers neatly on his desk in some semblance of order. Then he turned and left.

On the street he walked toward the share taxi. As he did so he stepped in to Quincallerie Uninet, a hardware store. He browsed up an aisle telling a worker he was just looking. He tried to walk slowly and examine a few items here and there before coming to the rope. Once there he saw it was on a big spool. He would have to ask someone to cut it at length. There would be small talk, questions, possibly suspicion. He walked up one more aisle picking up a painter's brush and returning it to the shelf before leaving. He still needed rope.

14

After stopping at the market for some food and another one liter water he moved toward the share taxis. He had to think of something but he also had to know if she and the baby were ok. His insides were in knots. If he could not before the share taxi arrived he would take her the food and water, return to his apartment, and find a solution there.

On the ride he went through his mind every store and vendor he could remember. It was not his normal stop and perhaps he was forgetting something. Perhaps there was a place? But where? Nothing came to mind.

The stop prior to his the share taxi pulled in to a small loading lane off the road. Two RPF soldiers stepped in to the share taxi. Faustin's heart began pounding as they scanned the seats. He knew in his mind that there was no way of them knowing his destination, but what if they began asking questions? What if they knew this was the wrong share taxi for his daily commute? It was late and these were dangerous days."

The soldiers pointed at the three people in the front bench seat. "Move back," one ordered. The three quickly shifted to the back of the Toyota minibus. Two found purchase of what little seat remained in the back two rows, pressing Faustin even closer to his neighbors. As they did he felt the scab on his side begin to seep. The third crouched in the small aisle and held to the shoulder of what must have been his wife.

At the next stop Faustin asked if he could exit. He stepped over his seatmate and the man in the aisle nervously stepped past the soldiers on to the roadway outside.

"You are bleeding!" his seatmate offered. "You have it on your shirt. On my shirt!"

Faustin stepped out of the share taxi. Having already paid upon entry he began to walk away with no intention of looking back.

"Stop!" one soldier commanded, "Stop!!"

Faustin froze. His hand went to his side impulsively. There was not a lot of blood but his shirt was certainly damp with stain where the scab peeled away.

"Where are you going?"

He turned to address the soldier. The other remained in the share taxi.

The soldier raised his AK47 rifle. "I asked where you were going?"

"Home sir. I – I – was at work late," Faustin managed to utter while turning back to face the soldier.

"Where do you live?"

"Kanombe."

"Kanombe?"

"Yes sir."

Faustin's fist tightened on his briefcase. The weight of Umimana's food seemed to double.

"This is not the right share taxi to get there. Where are you going?"

Faustin stuttered.

"I asked you a question? Why are you bleeding?"

In Faustin's mind he heard Ben Kayumba, "We have much work but it is not good to be out these days late. I hear several share taxis have even stopped running at night."

"Sir..." Faustin stumbled. The soldier moved his rifle subtly upward in a sign of aggression.

"Sir, Some share taxi's have stopped running at night. I take this one and walk because it is only one ride from my work. And this," Faustin gestured to his shirt, "I was caught on a thorn bush yesterday on my way home. It just reopened."

There was a moment pause. The soldier was deciding whether to press. A share taxi behind theirs honked, saw the soldiers, and made a gesture of apology. The one in front pulled slowly back on to the road only half loaded but eager to leave the ever-intensifying scene.

The standstill was broken not by the soldier but a cocky voice from a Toyota minibus parked a few meters ahead and off the road. The voice came from a man wearing a flat billed cap with Monica Lewinsky's face on it. His share taxi, all of them were decorated but this one was excessive, had "The Lewinsky" written large down the side with a caricature of Bill Clinton. Bill had his pants down, butt showing, and turning his head to flash a big thumbs up. It was perhaps the funniest share taxi art Faustin had seen. Looking at the soldier, Faustin believed he thought so as well.

The Lewensky's owner asserted, "He is right sir. I park my share taxi now. It isn't safe to drive at night. The damn cockroaches come out at night. I don't want any part of that."

The soldier smiled, "That they do, don't they?" He sneered, "The Cockroaches."

And with that the soldier turned and re-entered his share taxi.The driver, realizing motion was in his best interest, pulled away as soon as the soldier was seated.

Faustin realized he had not breathed. A gasp came from his pursed lips. A bead of sweat trickled from his eyebrow down his cheek.

"Murakoze, sir."

"Those damn soldiers are just kids. They are told to save bullets by using hatchets to kill people that used to teach them, sell them groceries, and hold them on their laps in my taxi."

He patted the Toyota minibus's side just beside Bill's backside, "I think they are strung to tight, about to snap from what they have been told to do. Most are willing to take any semi-good reason not to put more blood on their hands."

"Thank you none the less."

"Is your story true? You really making that walk through the woods?"

"Yes."

"You know there are..." the driver paused, searching for words to describe the killing fields, the pits, the darkness that resides so near their present location.

"These are dangerous days," Faustin offered.

The driver seemed relieved that his sentence would never have to be finished. "Yes they are. I hope you are heading straight home?"

Faustin looked at the driver. If there was anyone he could ask and not fear them telling the RPF Faustin thought it would be Mr. Monica Lewinsky cap. "Well," Faustin said, "I am after I figure out where to buy rope."

He waited for the driver to inquire but he only smiled. Faustin's gaze went from the man's eyes to his finger pointing and then to the top of The Lewinsky's roof.

A set of wood planks were on top attached by a length of rope. A good length. Long enough to tie to a woman's waist and pull her from a pit.

"Sir?"

"Yes."

"That rope? Is any of it for sale? Ummm... There is a... ummm.. there is a part of the trail... on my way home...."

The driver looked at Faustin intently. First his gaze on Faustin's eyes, checking his demeanor. Then slowly moved to the self-confessed thorn cut that shown bright red on his shirt. Then he returned to Faustin's eyes. "Well, I suppose they don't call it a share taxi for nothing. How much rope do you need?"

"All of it?" Faustin asked timidly.

"All of it?" Again, that intensive look. Faustin knew he was being searched and weighed. "That is a lot of rope to carry for a bit of difficult trail?"

Faustin began, "Well, there is..."

"No matter. I can put the lumber in my taxi. I'm done for the day. Take the rope."

"How much sir?"

"Best there be no transaction. As you say, these are dangerous days." The driver smiled.

"Murakoze sir. My name is..."

"There should be no need for that detail either," the man interrupted.

Faustin nodded with the understanding that this gentleman knew more than he would say but was a friend. Faustin helped him, in silence, take down the five sticks of lumber and place them in the share taxi under the bench seats. He then coiled the rope and began his way.

As he walked away the driver spoke a final word. It was a whispered voice though the message carried with clarity to Faustin's ears across the now still roadway stop. "Sir. If you should find the need. I do take one nighttime trip on Fridays. It is nonstop to Uganda. I will leave from here. Same time. Should you need such."

15

There was no answer at the pit when Faustin arrived and called her name. Faustin's heart was beating fast. He looked around to see if he was in ambush. Nothing. Darkness. The smell of death and rot. And no sound from his Uwimana. "Uwimana! Uwimana! Uwimana!!"

With each successive proclamation of her name he became louder, bolder, less cautious. "Uwimana!! Please! Answer!" Then he heard himself, "I can't! I can't!"

I can't what? Live without you? Ridiculous. He has never even seen her truly. Never seen her out of the darkness. And yet, he knew that was exactly wat his heart was saying.

Faustin began looking for something to fasten the rope to so he could descend, even at risk of being trapped himself. He would go down and find her. He must find her. And he prayed she would be alive.

As he was looking to tether the rope he heard, "Faustin? Faustin?"

"YES! Yes! Uwimana! It is I!"

He saw her stir. A hand placed to her lips. "Shhh…"

"Yes," he reduced his voice to a whisper. "Are you alright? Your child?"

"I am weak."

"Can you loop the rope? Hold your child?"

"I must, mustn't I?"

"I fear so... my love."

The words hung. Faustin felt them go out, enter the abyss, reach the bottom, and settle on Uwimana. There was no regret. They were his words and he meant them.

"Murakoze."

Faustin began tying a loop in each end. One for his waist and one for hers.

"Faustin?"

He would get her to place the loop around her.

"Yes Uwimana?"

He would pull using all his might to hoist her and child up the pit's wall.

"Is it odd?"

He knew he would struggle, fall, grasp for traction.

"Is what odd?"

He would expend himself in the effort more so than any work he had ever engaged in his sedentary lifestyle.

"Is it odd that I love you too."

But he would raise her from this place, from the prospect of a certain death. She would walk again but next time in his arms. And together they would find less dangerous days.

Two Blown Tires Means Road Trip

(A letter to a friend)

Riley C. Shannon

2 May 2002 (or thereabouts)

I am taking a couple of days off from work because the guy I'm married to (that's what I call him. His name is actually Dean) has gone home to Kentucky to see his mom. I was going to work around the house, but I have, as usual, come to a standstill because the whole thing is completely overwhelming. I don't know where to begin, so I stopped and came to Hugo (my computer) and decided I'd type on this missive to you for a while.

(Along about here is where I got shanghaied and wound up in the weekend from hell. The following will give you an idea of what my life has been like since about 1985, which is when the guy I'm married to moved in with me.)

Maybe I should just start this thing over from here… sort of… and tell you about *the weekend from hell!*

It all started Wednesday, when Dean went to Kentucky to see his mom. I had just bought him a car a couple of weeks ago because he doesn't like to look for cars. So, because I'm the one who does the homework and plays the car buying game, I am the elected official car buyer in the house. I picked him out a nice 1996 Nissan Sentra GXE. It had some things that needed work. Those things were corrected. Dean is in his "new" car now (it replaced a 1991 Ford Tempo that was dying a lingering death). He decided to go to Kentucky (that's where he's from, originally) and he's in his Sentra and everything is fine. *Until* he starts home on Saturday. That's when all hell breaks loose.

Understand something here: I was raised to be very independent. I didn't really want to get married. Mine is a marriage of convenience. Dean wanted social acceptance and I wanted medical insurance. know it sounds mercenary, but it's worked so far. However, I didn't take him to raise, and that's what it feels like, and it gets worse every day. I want *him* to be independent and be able to handle things on his own, but it's not happening. Therefore, when something goes wrong, he calls me. It doesn't matter what it is. *I am the (wo)man.*

So, he calls Saturday morning at around 9:45 to tell me he's on his way home. Fine. Julian (my friend who lives at my house because I'm charitable and his stepfather's an abusive alcoholic) and I are sitting at the computers when the phone rings and its Dean on the other end, yelling "*I need help and I need it NOW!!!* He's at a pay phone, on the Tennessee/Kentucky state line, screaming that he's blown two tires and he wants me to fix it *now*. Yes, but I don't have a magic wand to wave and make the tires inflate, and I am three hours away, so *now* is quite impossible. There is no calming him down. I ask him where he is and he tells me he's at Chubby's Amaco in Orlinda, Tennessee (where is that?) and no one will help him (and don't you just love those country names for service stations which aren't really service stations but convenience stores without mechanics?). I tell him to go inside and ask the lady (who is scared witless by now) what her phone number is so I can call her and maybe find out who might be able to help him. He hangs up on me. I call the Tennessee Highway Patrol and the woman on the other end of the phone says, "This is Chattanooga." I say, "Yeah, but you guys have branches all over the state, right?" She tells me she can't help me, but gives me the number to TDOT. I call that number. "This is Chattanooga." "Yeah, but you guys have trucks that go all over the state, right?" They give me the number for Nashville. I call them. "We don't go outside Davidson County." (Why do I think that's so much bull, since I see those trucks all over the state?) I am getting nowhere.

I called information to get the number for Chubby's Amaco. I called up there and said, "Is there a crazy man there? I'm looking for him. I'm married to him."

The lady on the other end of the phone said, "Oh, Hon, I am so sorry. I'm worried about him. He took off out of here and I had to call the police. He's crazy."

I said, "Yes, I know. But he's not dangerous to anyone but himself."

She said, "Hon, he's gone, and I'm worried about him. He took off walking back to his car justa yellin' and hollerin'. And he hung up on the only guy around here who does tires on Saturday." (Lesson: *Never* hang up on the *only* guy from the middle of nowhere who does tires on a Saturday.)

I said, "Okay. You say you called the police? Can you tell

me who you called or give me a number to call?"

She gave me the number to the Robertson County Sheriff's Department. I called them and said, "I'm looking for my husband. You've probably got a call on him from Chubby's Amaco. He's acting a little crazy."

The officer said, "Yeah, we're trying to find him now."

I told the officer, "They said he was walking back to the car".

"We can't find him."

"The car is on 65. Right past the Tennessee Welcome Center."

"We haven't found it."

"Well, he's headed that way. He's depressed and mad because he's got two flat tires and he says no one will help him so he's acting crazy, but he's not dangerous to anyone but himself. "

"Does he have medication?"

"He's on Prozac weekly, but I don't know the last time he took it. Now, he's a head-banger…."

"Yeah, we know about that. The lady at Chubby's said he was banging his head on the counter and the gas pumps."

"Uh, yeah, that would be him. Could you guys call me when you find him so I can figure out what to do about him and the car?"

"Yeah, sure thing. What's your number?"

I gave them my number and started the next phase of strategic planning, which was what to grab on short notice, because it's looking like a road trip. And it's raining.

The sheriff's office calls. They have him in their lobby and will hold him there until we come get him.

Julian and I threw some things in a duffle bag, and started grabbing tools. We got the car loaded up with the gear and started out of town. We stopped at Julian's brother's shop (Joe is a mechanic) for a tire plug kit, a portable air tank, and some other tools. We think we're pretty much set at this point, and know that Joe can haul the car back on the rollback if we can't get it fixed. So, we're off, stuck with whatever radio stations we can pick up along the way because we forgot the requisite road trip music. But we'll survive.

We stopped in South Pittsburg for Krystals, which you can eat while you drive. I drive and eat and we have interesting conversations and speculate as to how he flattened two tires. We got to Nashville, and the interstate was a parking lot, so we took Briley Parkway to get around it and hit I-65 headed toward Louisville. We found the exit where we needed to get off and Julian started trying to read the directions to Springfield that I wrote down in a hurried scribble which even I can't read. He managed to make it out (I think he's secretly some sort of CIA cryptographer or something).

We drove and drove and drove until the word 'drove' started sounding funny. Springfield is in the boonies, and I kept wondering if we were lost, but we eventually ran into it. We called the sheriff's office to find out where to go, got directions, and found the building. We were on the wrong side of it (the jail side) and had to call them again so they could tell us to walk around the building. We found the sheriff's office and here comes Dean, all sulking and sad. I was very blasphemous at this point when I said, "All right, here's the deal. Right now, I am God, (pointing to Julian) this is Jesus Christ, and we're here to save your ass (I was really mad)."

Dean said, "What about Kitty (my cat)?" I told him, "Do you see Kitty? No. Kitty is the Holy Ghost. Now, where's the car?"

We went inside the Sheriff's office to see if the dispatcher could tell me exactly where the car is but, for once, Dean knows exactly where it is, so we just needed directions to I-65. The officer gave us directions and we were on the road again, driving until we crossed into Kentucky, at which point we realized we'd made a wrong turn. We doubled back, found our turnoff, and finally hit the interstate.

I spotted the car before anyone else did. It was on the shoulder of the interstate. I wasn't in a position to try to take one of those "authorized vehicles only" turnarounds, so we had to go up to the Franklin, Kentucky exit and turn around. We got back to the car and, sure enough, both tires on the driver's side were damaged. The back tire was flat, but the front tire was still inflated just enough to drive on it. The front rim was bent so badly that it was pinching the hubcap between it and the tire. The hubcap was sticking out almost parallel to the ground like those blade things you see on Roman chariot wheels in old movies. I broke the hubcap when I pulled it off the wheel. The bend in the rim was, however, actually holding air in the tire because when I tried to inflate it later, it almost blew up.

Julian pulled the back tire off and put the doughnut on in its place. We figured the front tire would get us a little ways. Our goal was to put two doughnuts on it, Dean's and the one out of my car, and then drive it somewhere to get help, but that didn't work out. Dean's car has 13 inch wheels and mine has 15 inchers. I didn't realize that as we were pulling out of the driveway or I'd have gotten the doughnut out of my 94 Sentra.

Julian managed to get the doughnut on the car without any of us getting hit by a speeding transfer truck. I stood on the side of the road in a white T-shirt warding the vehicles away from us. It helps that I'm a large woman because when cars and trucks see me, they think twice about being in a position where they might hit me because I'm gonna make a BIG dent. And I have perfected that "I'm-going-dent-your- car-*so-bad*" look when crossing the street. So, I stood there and warned Julian when I thought a vehicle was too close to us. I had to tell Dean to back away from the road and the car. He was trying to see what was going on with the repairs and he kept getting in the way and sticking his head out into traffic.

Julian got the tire changed out and we all headed south so we could get off the interstate to a safer place to do more work on the car. We got off at Orlinda, where Chubby's Amaco is, and pulled into Chubby's parking lot. Dean opted to stay in the car since Chubby's was where he made such a scene. Julian switched out the damaged front tire with the good rear tire because we were going to have to drive back up the interstate to Franklin as that's where the Wal-Mart was located. We hoped to get tires there. Julian didn't want to have a front tire blow out while driving since that really screws up your steering capabilities. We drove back up to Franklin on a back road, which ran parallel to the interstate, and found the Super Wal-Mart, but the tire shop was closed. It was going to be Sunday morning before we could do anything. We got a room at Best Western and I dropped Dean and a bag of McDonald's burgers off there and went back to the Wal-Mart to confer with Julian about our next move. A lady in Wal-Mart had called Flying J for us, but they didn't do tires. They did give us the numbers for three companies that did do emergency road service, so Julian called the numbers and was told that one company had four in front of us and one had seven, but Bubba's Truck Repair ("Don't cuss, call us!") could be there in an hour and a half, so we went with Bubba's. Rick and Pete showed up and brought a couple of Goodyear tires with them. Pete took one look at the damaged tires and said, "He's hit a curb." When I told him it had happened coming out of the welcome center, Pete said, "That ain't the first time that's happened." They changed the tires out, but when they went to put the rear tire on, two of the lug studs stripped, and they weren't opposing studs. You can drive a car on two opposing studs, but not on two right next to each other, so we were pretty much screwed until the next morning when they could go to Auto Zone or Advanced and get some studs.

Pete looked like a pirate, and I imagined him with an eye patch and an earring. His voice was like the one Billy Bob Thornton used in "Sling Blade", but he talked fast and sort of mumbled. "Now yew kin drive 'at car wi'them two studs, but yew 'on't git far withem lahk 'at so ah wouldn't. Nope, wouldn't recommendit atall. Wheel'll fly right offat recommend it here." I didn't want to drive it like that anyway, so they left it sitting on a block of wood in the Wal-Mart parking lot in Franklin, Kentucky for the night. It was now midnight.

Julian and I went back to the room and we all got ready for bed. Dean was so agitated that he was bouncing around all over the bed, and I don't sleep with him anyway, so Julian and I bunked together while Dean practiced levitation and spinning in the air all night. If I had slept over there, I'd have been beaten to death by morning, the way he was flailing around.

Sunday was a pretty day, nice and sunny, not too hot. We all went for the continental breakfast and I called Bubba's to see when we needed to meet them about the car. Checkout was at 11:00, and no one called to tell us to meet them, so we checked out and went back to the Wal-Mart. We found that Rick had been waiting for about 45 minutes for us to show up. I said, "Pete told me he'd call me when you guys were ready for us. I gave him the number to the hotel, but he never called." Rick said, "I'm gonna kick his ass when I get back to the shop," and I don't doubt that he did.

Rick put the tire on the car and presented me with the bill: $284.09. This was an expensive trip for Dean, who swears he's never going back to Kentucky. He's said before that he was never going back somewhere when something bad happened. (He once got a speeding ticket in Red Bank. He screamed, "I'm never going to set foot in Red Bank ever again!!!" I chuckled and said, "Yeah, right. You *live* in Red Bank, you idiot."). And that bill doesn't include the $60 for the hotel room, the gas it took me to get up there, the new rim ($55), new hubcaps ($44), switching out the rims, balancing the tires, replacement of any other missing or stripped lug studs, and a front end alignment. And I am expected to take care of all the stuff that's left to be done to the car.

It was a long, somewhat silent, drive back home. Julian drove Dean's car and Dean rode with me. We weren't about to let him drive back after this fiasco. Now Dean is driving my 94 Sentra and his car is at NTB having all the leftover work done on it. I want him out of my car as soon as possible. He has a tendency to hit things and not tell you, which is why the bumper on my 94 is bowed out and the trunk deck is warped. He backed into something in it.

So, you wonder what I've been up to for the last 20 or so years and incidents like this are pretty much what my life has been like. You had said your life was pretty much Norman Rockwell and I said mine was Edvard Munch. What immediately popped into my head when you said Norman Rockwell was Munch's "The Scream". That's my life, on canvas. I try to see the humor in everything. I have to laugh or I'll go completely insane. Sometimes, I think I'm walking right on the edge of sanity/insanity. Sometimes, if I stand on one foot, I'm in both worlds.

NTB called about the car. It'll be around $450 to fix it and they're going to have to do a "sub-frame shift" which basically tells me the frame is bent. It's a uni-body construction car, which means it's actually totaled. But I just bought the dang thing, so he'll live with it, even if it does go down the road like a crab.

About The Authors

Calvin Beam

Calvin Beam was born in Philadelphia and received his bachelor of journalism degree from the University of Missouri. He survived a 30-plus year newspaper career with his sense of humor intact, although the same cannot be said for his retirement account. He lives in Chattanooga, Tenn., where the pace of Southern life suits him just fine.

Elijah David

Elijah David lives and works in the Chattanooga area. He spends far too many nights reading when he should be sleeping and frequently finds his bookshelves have shrunk overnight. He is the author of Albion Academy, the first book in the Albion Quartet, and his stories and poems have appeared in publications from The Crossover Alliance, Oloris Publishing, and Troy University's Rubicon.Though his only magical talent is putting pen to paper, Elijah believes magic lurks around every corner, if you only know how to look for it. He and his wife are busy raising a small Hobbit and a calico cat. Elijah David can be found online at

    elijahdavidauthor.blogspot.com

    facebook/elijahdavidauthor

    goodreads.com/author/show/14746895.Elijah_David

Gary Sedlacek

Gary Sedlacek and his wife live near Chattanooga, TN. He has submitted here a chapter from "Burnished Obsidian", his novel about people in the Midwest resolving themselves against a background of economic and social change.

J. Smith Kirkland

J. Smith Kirkland grew up in a haunted house in Dallas Bay, TN. This probably contributes to the fact that his fictional stories revolve around fate, ghosts, witches, and legends. His "Tales of the Catalin" series can be found on Amazon along with his essays in collections like "Growing Up Without WiFi."

Jerry Harwood

Jerry is married and has six children. He has worked six different jobs including Camp Director, College Professor, Restaurant owner, CADCII Counselor and Program Director, and Middle School Teacher. You'll have to ask about the sixth one. For a third set of six, Jerry has been blessed with a plethora of life experiences including traveling extensively to Rwanda in the late 90's, teaching at a communist university in Ukraine, backpacking Europe, being an honorary member of the Black Student Union in college, being accepted as a member of a women's theological group, and he was once a dues paying girl scout. In his spare time he pursues the hobbies of being a volunteer fireman and writing.

Joe Petrie

Joe Petree's short stories capture the special meanings of everyday moments. A prolific writer who created a number of thriller and Western novellas, he was a wonderful mentor, and a longtime member of the Chattanooga Writers Guild and this critique group. An Army veteran, and a retired engineer, he was a lifelong learner and sharer. Joe died in 2017.

Kelle Z. Riley

Kelle Z. Riley, writer, speaker, global traveler, Ph.D. chemist and safety/martial arts expert has been featured in public forums that range from local newspapers to national television. In addition to her works of fiction, a personal story was included in "Chicken Soup for the Soul: Living with Alzheimer's and Other Dementias." Her other publications include a romantic suspense (Dangerous Affairs), multiple short stories, a self-published memoire in honor of her father, and the newly released Undercover Cat Series books: "The Cupcake Caper," "Shaken, Not Purred," and "The Tiger's Tale," which feature a scientist-turned-sleuth. A former Golden Heart Finalist, Kelle resides in Chattanooga, TN. She is the past program chair and popular speaker for the Chattanooga Writer's Guild, a member of Sisters in Crime, Romance Writers' of America and various local chapters. When not writing, she can be found pursuing passions such as being a self-defense instructor, a Master Gardener Intern and a full time chemist with numerous professional publications and U. S. patents. Kelle can be reached at

facebook.com/kellyzriley, twitter.com/kellezriley, kellezriley.net

Marcus Brian Bankstone

Marcus Brian Bankstone has lived in the Chattanooga, Tennessee area all his life. He has been a computer programmer and technician.

He is rather shy and guarded to the outside world. He's a natural pessimist with a self-imposed drive towards optimism and hope.

This is his first venture into the literary world.

Riley C. Shannon

Riley C. Shannon was born and raised in the Hixson, Tennessee area. She has written poetry, stories, and journal entries all her life.

She loves the word "snarky", and tries to see the humor in everything. This is the first time any of her writing has ever been published.

Meredith Hodges-Boos

The book cover was created by Meredith Hodges-Boos, who is a writer in the group and the author and illustrator of children books. https://www.rabbit-feathers.com

Made in the USA
Columbia, SC
09 February 2022